ISBN 978-1-330-96634-1
PIBN 10127412

This book is a reproduction of an important historical work. Forgotten Books uses
state-of-the-art technology to digitally reconstruct the work, preserving the original format
whilst repairing imperfections present in the aged copy. In rare cases, an imperfection in
the original, such as a blemish or missing page, may be replicated in our edition. We do,
however, repair the vast majority of imperfections successfully; any imperfections that
remain are intentionally left to preserve the state of such historical works.

1 MONTH OF
FREE
READING

at
www.ForgottenBooks.com

By purchasing this book you are eligible for one month membership to ForgottenBooks.com, giving you unlimited access to our entire collection of over 700,000 titles via our web site and mobile apps.

To claim your free month visit:
www.forgottenbooks.com/free127412

English
Français
Deutsche
Italiano
Español
Português

www.forgottenbooks.com

Mythology Photography **Fiction**
Fishing Christianity **Art** Cooking
Essays Buddhism Freemasonry
Medicine **Biology** Music **Ancient
Egypt** Evolution Carpentry Physics
Dance Geology **Mathematics** Fitness
Shakespeare **Folklore** Yoga Marketing
Confidence Immortality Biographies
Poetry **Psychology** Witchcraft
Electronics Chemistry History **Law**
Accounting **Philosophy** Anthropology
Alchemy Drama Quantum Mechanics
Atheism Sexual Health **Ancient History**
Entrepreneurship Languages Sport
Paleontology Needlework Islam
Metaphysics Investment Archaeology
Parenting Statistics Criminology
Motivational

Return this book on or before the
Latest Date stamped below.

University of Illinois Library

PHOTO THE SULIOTE.

LONDON :
Printed by G. BARCLAY, Castle St. Leicester Sq.

PHOTO THE SULIOTE

A Tale of Modern Greece.

By DAVID R. MORIER, Esq.

IN THREE VOLUMES.

VOL. III.

LONDON:
L. BOOTH, 307 REGENT STREET.

PHOTO THE SULIOTE.

CHAPTER XXXV.

WHEN Angelica recovered from the swoon in which she was left by Alỳ Pasha, she found herself in a strange place, surrounded by faces equally strange, of women all busied in her service.

She was perfectly unconscious of what had happened in the interval, and now, although partially reinstated in the possession of her senses, was still so bewildered with the confused recollection of the scene she had witnessed, that the new objects actually present to her appeared to be but the continuation of a dream.

Her eyes wandered vaguely from one

side to another, as if seeking some explanation at the hands of the attendants, who, as she began gradually to comprehend, had been very zealously employed in stripping her of her wayfaring garments, preparatory to her passing into the Hammam.

Angelica was, in fact, surrounded by the female slaves in the service of the harem, attendants on the Pashina, and the room into which she had been removed was no other but the antechamber, or unrobing room, of the private bath, which formed a part of the building of the seraï, and was devoted to the use of the Vezir's domestic establishment.

Among the attendants was an ancient dame, who directed the service of the younger menials with an authority of command which repressed all giggling and familiarity.

Few words were spoken, and these in a low whisper; but, as Angelica listened, the remarks which struck her ear thoroughly roused her to full consciousness, and awakened the utmost alarm as to the issue of the perilous adventure she found herself engaged in.

" *Vallah, güzel tchok!*—By Heaven! what a lovely creature it is!—What eyes! —What a shape!—Her hair is like the finest Broussa silk. She is worthy to be *Cadinn* in chief* of the Padishah."

All these compliments, and many more which were uttered in the bath, and while her toilet, on her emersion from the steam, was carried on in the adjoining apartment under the inspection of the old lady before mentioned, were listened to in anxious silence by poor Angelica, whose gratification at the praises lavished on her personal charms, had she been touched by them, was more than counterbalanced by the suspicions which those praises raised in her bosom, that all this was preliminary to some purpose of the Pasha's, either to keep her captive in his harem, or to send her as a present to the Sultan.

* *Vide* Note.

Indeed, no one who had seen Yanko's lovely wife, as she was led by the old crone into an inner chamber, the most splendidly furnished of the harem, but must have acknowledged her rightful claim, like the successor of Queen Vashti in the eyes of King Ahasuerus, to be preferred above all her competitors for the royal favour.

Whatever could heighten the effect of beauty in the way of dress, according to the fashion of the country, had been carefully arranged by the mistress of the robes. The gauze chemisette,—the silken under-vest, fastened at the waist with a row of innumerable small silk buttons, open at the sleeves,—the upper garment of the finest shawl, richly embroidered with gold thread,—the girdle with its massive silver clasps,—the diamond jewel on the light embroidered cap, gracefully placed on one side, from which streamed in silky waves a profusion of the most luxuriant auburn tresses.

All this apparatus,—the artillery employed by Beauty for the destruction of the heedless gazers who venture within range of eye-shot,—only served as a foil to the surpassing comeliness of Angelica, whose charm resided in the inborn grace of that artless, childlike purity of look and manner, which awes, while it fascinates, the beholder.

Angelica was conducted with a degree of marked deference and official ceremony to the place of honour in the upper corner of the divan, which only increased her uneasiness; when to her delight, no less than to her extreme surprise, on the retreat of the old lady and the other attendants who had accompanied her into the room, there slipped in from behind the perdèh her faithful Arghyrousa.

If the reader asks, How did she, a stranger, find means to penetrate into the innermost recesses of a three-tailed Pasha's harem? I must answer him by another question: Did he ever hear of any contrivance or invention by which a woman, bent on obtaining the settled purpose of her heart, be that purpose for good or for ill, was to be prevented from accomplishing it? Could he ever keep out from his house a strange cat that had a mind to get into it?

"Never mind how I came here, Kyrà-mou," answered Arghyrousa, to the inquiring and delighted look of her mistress. "I am here to share your fate, whatever it may be. I have seen and heard enough to know that you are in the midst of dangers of various kinds; but, with God's help and the blessed Panayïa's, we will escape them all. When you hear the Muezzin's chant from that minaret you are to expect a visit from the Vezir."

At this announcement Angelica turned deadly pale. Clasping her hands, she faintly said, "God protect me!" Then, hastily rising from her seat, "Let us fly, Arghyroúsamou! I will set out instantly for Kalarýtes, and never will I again stir

from home. I have done what my husband bade me do. My duty is fulfilled.
What more can the Vezir want with me?
Why have I been tricked out in all this
finery? Let us go!" she passionately
repeated, and with trembling hands attempted to detach from her dress the
jewels with which she had been so carefully adorned.

But Arghyrousa gently repressed her.
"Sweet mistress mine, I entreat you to
be calm. It is in vain to attempt escaping
now. A,thousand eyes are on the watch.
All this has been done by the Pasha's
directions. Resume the seat of honour
which has been assigned to you by his
express command; and when he comes,
be sure you betray no suspicion of any
evil designs."

Poor Angelica! Ardently as she longed
to have the wings of a dove, that she
might flee away and be at rest, she felt
that she had hardly the strength to move
across the room. She yielded, perforce,

to the remonstrance of her faithful servant,—now her only friend,—and being
again seated, bent over Arghyrousa, who
sat on the floor at her feet. "Tell me,"
she said, "what is become of *him*? The
last I saw of——" Her lips, quivering
with horror at the recollection of what
she had last seen of Photo, refused to give
utterance to her thought.

"Photo lives!" replied Arghyrousa.
"There is no question, for the present,
of his execution; and but for you, dearest mistress, the poor lad would now have
been a corpse floating on the lake, or
cast on the shore to be devoured by
jackals."

This assurance, that she had been the
means of snatching the life of a fellow-
creature from destruction, revived the
fainting spirit of Angelica. The gush of
adoring gratitude, which found its way in
a flood of tears, swept away all her despondency and all her alarms.

"Thank God!" she fervently exclaimed,

"thank God for this great mercy! And now," she said, turning to Arghyrousa, "tell me all you know, all you have learnt, since we parted this morning."

"You remember that mad Dervish," said Arghyrousa, "whom we fell in with on the road as we came down the mountain?"

"Yes; what of him?"

"Well, he is no more a Dervish than I am. He is a true man, dear mistress, as this will prove to you;" and Arghyrousa put into Angelica's hand the lock of hair, which she recognised as the same she had given to her unknown visitor at Kalarýtes. "The man who sends you this is at hand, for no other purpose but at the hazard of his own life to save you and the Suliote boy from the perils which encompass you both."

"Who and what is he? How came you to meet him, and where?" eagerly inquired Angelica.

Arghyrousa proceeded thus to satisfy her mistress's curiosity :—

" When you, Kyràmou, refused to let your unworthy handmaid share the perils of your visit to this den, I went, according to your orders, straight to ´Kyr Yanko's house ; and when I had opened the street-door with the key which I luckily thought of bringing with me from Kalarýtes, before I had time to close it, who should follow me into the court but the same Dervish! Well, knowing the cool impudence of these saintly vagabonds, I was prepared for his demanding something for his convent ; but as I was not in a humour to submit to any extortion of the kind, I made up my mind to a strife of tongues, in which I knew I could be his match, before getting rid of him. But I was alarmed on seeing him deliberately bolt the street-door. This foreboded violence ; but I was not more disposed to receive blows from such a beggar, than I was to give him money. So I snatched up a

broken plank which lay on the ground,
and told him that if he did not unbolt the
door that instant, and be off to his convent, I would break it upon his head;
and I lifted up the plank with both hands
to be as good as my word.

"At this menace the man exclaimed,
'*El' humd 'ul illah!*' Then, throwing
down his Dervish's cap, burst into a loud
laugh, and added in good Greek,—

"'Thou art the girl for me! Now I
see that I can depend upon thee, Arghyrousa.' How the old man came to know
my name, I can't guess.

"He continued (but now in a grave and
serious tone):—'Arghyrousa, lovest thou
thy mistress? Wilt thou risk thy life for
her?'

"'That will I,' said I, 'any day.'"
Angelica here interrupted the narrative
by an affectionate kiss on Arghyrousa's
cheek.

"'I believe thee, my daughter; the

flash of thine eye tells me thou art one
. of the faithful. Thy mistress is now, as
Daniel was, in the den of lions; nay, in a
worse plight than he, in as far as a brutal
Turk is worse than a brute beast. But
God will be with her; for she is in the
path of duty, and so has nothing to fear.
In saving her husband's life, she saves
also that of the brave young Suliote. Yet
it is by instruments that God acts, and
thou art appointed to assist in the rescue
of thy mistress from the peril she has not
hesitated to encounter at the bidding of a
stranger. Do thou go to the seraï; gain
admission to her, and do not leave her
side for an instant. Give her this;' and
he pulled from his bosom that token.
' Tell her, Samuel the Caloyero is true
to his word, and is here watching for
her safety and Photo's. There's no time
to lose. I must be gone. But remember,' and he picked up his bonnet, which
he replaced on his head, ' I am still the

Delhi Dervish. Now put on a veil and féréjé, and make the best of thy way to the seraï. Thou wilt not be noticed among the crowds going to see the execution of Photo, from which I am going, *Inshallah!* to rescue him. The passages are all open to the women who have dealings with the harem. Follow them, as if thou wert one of them; and, by the favour of the Panayïa and thy own wit, thou wilt find access to thy mistress. Keep thy own counsel. Have all thy eyes and ears about thee; and if thou canst, hold thy woman's tongue. God be with us, and spare us all at the judgment-day!' "

Arghyrousa had hardly done speaking when the chant of the Muezzin was heard, and immediately after the perdèh was lifted up by the old mistress of ceremonies, who announced the approach of the Vezir, and then withdrew, to go and inform his Highness that all was ready for his reception.

A shudder came over Angelica at the announcement.

"Fear not, dearest mistress," said Arghyrousa; "we'll be a match for them all yet. Look at me," continued she in a whisper, as the sound of many steps in the passage was heard. "Remember that I am an idiot, deaf and dumb, and very mischievous withal, out of your sight."

Angelica looked on her attendant's face, which had assumed such a dull, stupid expression, that she could scarcely believe she had not been metamorphosed into some other person.

At that instant Alỳ Pasha entered the room. Angelica rose to receive him, and he unceremoniously assumed the seat she had left, without apparently taking any notice of her.

She stood before him for a few moments, in a state of the most embarrassing suspense as to whether she ought to address him first, or wait his speaking. Her embarrassment grew into alarm as, looking up, she became conscious that the gaze of the despot was fixed admiringly upon her; there was a flush on his cheek, and a twinkle in his keen, cruel eye, which betrayed the intemperance of the meal he had lately finished. She felt like the dove within reach of the talons of the obscene kite, painfully conscious that she was now delivered up, with all her natural attractions adorned and garlanded, as it were, for the sacrifice, into the power of the unscrupulous tyrant.

Angelica could not doubt the meaning of that gaze, when Alỳ, suddenly perceiving the presence of Arghyrousa, who had placed herself at the end of the room, a few paces behind her mistress, he exclaimed, in a shrill, angry tone,—

"That woman! who is she? What business hast thou here, woman?" continued he, addressing himself to Arghyrousa. "Begone!"

Arghyrousa stood immovable in the same spot, as if quite unconscious of being

the object of the Vezir's observation. She
looked at him in the face, but with the
sleepy, unmeaning stare, of a crazy simpleton, the air of whom she had assumed
with such imperturbable composure and
perfect *naturel*, that Angelica, who turned
her eyes upon her as Alỳ spoke, could
hardly believe that her sharp-witted maid
had not actually turned idiot with fright
at the position they were both in.

The Pasha, now addressing himself to
Angelica in a still more impatient tone,
repeated the question,—

"Who is that deaf idiot? Bid her begone!"

"Sir," said Angelica, endeavouring to
conceal her growing apprehensions by the
assumed calmness of her manner, "she
is my serving-woman—a poor simpleton
afflicted with deafness, as your Highness
says.   But she is a faithful creature; she
accompanied me from Kalarỳtes, whither
it is time for me to return, and, with your
permission, we will now both be gone."

So saying, Yanko's wife made her obeisance, with the same bashful grace with which she first received the Vezir at his entrance; and, making a sign to Arghyrousa to move, was about quitting the chamber, when the peremptory command of Alỳ Pasha, while he half rose from his seat, compelled her to pause.

"Not yet; I can't let you depart yet, Kyrà Angelica," continued he, in a less harsh tone; then, observing the paleness of her cheek, in which mental alarm and physical weakness had an equal share, he, perhaps fearing another swoon, now courteously invited her to be seated—an invitation which her trembling limbs, with no consent of her mind, were glad to obey.

Angelica took her seat at the other extremity of the divan, of which the corner was occupied by the Vezir; and Arghyrousa, without waiting for invitation or bidding, placed herself on the floor at the feet of her mistress, whose hand she held between hers, gently smoothing and kissing it, as if to give her courage. All this she did with a look so vacant and silly, that the Pasha, heeding her no more than a tame, dozing cat, resumed the conversation with Angelica, which, as we have seen, the events of the early morning had so suddenly interrupted.

"You think me to be a bad man," said he, in such a tone as the wolf might assume when trying to pass off for a lamb. "When you know me better, you will not think me so. The man you saw me shoot this morning, *he* was a bad man, indeed. And it was for *your* sake that I was obliged to kill him at that moment. If I had not, your journey to put this letter into my hands would have been in vain."

Here he took from his bosom Yanko's missive to his wife, with its Klephtic postscript, of which Angelica had been the bearer.

The Vezir, who keenly watched the

varying expression of Angelica's face as he spake, to ascertain the effect which it was his object to produce in her breast, continued,—

" You know the conditions upon which your husband can alone escape the fate those Klephts threaten him with. His life against that Suliote Klephtopoulo's life—that is their bargain. Now, tell me the truth, Kyrà, should you be very unhappy if you never saw that husband of yours again ?"

This abrupt question, which betrayed the working of evil thoughts in the mind of the interrogator, produced in that of Angelica the same startling shock which they experience who find themselves suddenly on the edge of an eddying current, within sight of breakers, on a lee shore. The look which accompanied the question left no doubt of its meaning.

The sensual Turk had yet to learn what strength there is in the innocent and chaste heart resolved to pursue, under all difficulties, the safe, though rugged, path of duty.

Angelica replied,—" Had I been indifferent to my husband's fate, as your Highness's question implies, I should not have dared to intrude into your presence to-day. I beseech you, in your clemency, to consider the danger his life is exposed to by delay. He is a faithful servant of my Lord the Vezir, who would surely take no pleasure in seeing a wife reduced to the helpless state of a widow. It is affliction enough for me to have come, an orphan child, into a strange land ——"

The sense of her forlorn condition, such as it might become if aggravated by the bereavement even of such a protector as her unworthy husband, brought tears into the eyes of Angelica, which only the more inflamed the rising passion of her formidable admirer.

He continued in the same strain of cruel bantering, regardless of feelings which his own coarse nature, and the habits of despotic sway, incapacitated him to comprehend.

"Oh, as for your widowhood, that need not last long! I would engage to provide you with a fresh husband—not so ugly as Yanko, nor so good-for-nothing a villain as you, Kyrà, have good reason to know him to be."

Angelica trembled from head to foot as she heard this strange language, which, whatever might be her own inward sense of the demerits of her husband, she, as a wife, felt it to be a crime to listen to.

Dreading the continuance of an interview which she anticipated could only end in some outrage on the part of the Pasha, who was evidently deep in his cups, Angelica made a movement to rise from her seat, with the intention of quitting the room and rushing forth, she hardly knew whither.

This the Pasha rudely repressed, by suddenly placing his hand upon her shoulder, and commanding her in a peremptory voice not to stir.

"Listen to me, woman!" said he, in the same shrill tone which had caused her such terror at her first interview in the morning; "you have made a journey hither to deliver me this filthy scrap of paper, and you would make me believe that you are only desirous to save the life of your *husband!* But think you that *I* am to be so deceived? Do not I know that you were in league with the Klephts, and that your real object is to obtain by his exchange the life of that Suliote vermin—that Photo? 'Tis *he* you care for! Yes, wife of Yanko! you may well change colour. I know what you women are made of. He is truly a handsome youth. No wonder you would prefer him to that bull-faced Vlackh you call your husband. Yes, your blushes speak it. Now hear me, wife of Yanko! it depends on you to save the Suliote's head. You

start!—hear me. The condition is a very
simple one. Let him only enter my service, and receive my pay, as other Palikaria do, and from that moment his life is
safe. He has nothing to expect from his
own people. His own father and mother
have cast him off. Let not his pride
stand in the way of his acceptance of an
offer which secures not only his life, but
enjoyment such as his bare mountains
never could afford. Do you, Kyrà Angelica, propose this to the youth—he will
not resist *your* persuasion, and thus your
journey will not have been in vain."

Angelica heard this proposal like one
in a dream. Before she could well comprehend its meaning the Pasha added, in
a tone that roused her from her bewilderment to an agonising sense of the responsibility thus unexpectedly thrust upon
her,—

" He must make his choice instantly,
or he will not see the light of another sun.
You shall ere long have the opportunity

to exert your influence. If the boy perish, his blood be on thy head, thou
wife—then widow—of Yanko."

So saying, the Vezir rose from his seat
and left the room.

As long as the tread of his step along
the gallery, which connected the apartments of the harem with the· rest of the
seraï, was within hearing, Arghyrousa
preserved her attitude and look of an
idiot, as though fearing to be detected in
a lucid interval by the Pasha, whom she
had so well succeeded in deceiving. But
no sooner was she assured, by the silence
which prevailed after his departure, that
there was no danger of his sudden return,
than resuming her natural expression of
manner, and starting on her feet, she exclaimed,—

" *Oof!* that mad Dervish can't accuse
me of not knowing how to hold my woman's tongue. I may now speak out,
praised be the blessed Panayïa!—Well,
after all, the Vezir is not such a hard

man as people say he is. Surely Photaki
will make no difficulty to save his head
upon the easy terms of eating the Turk's
salt, and wearing a clean shirt. You,
Kyràmou, will of course recommend his
acceptance of so fair an offer, and he will
certainly follow any advice you give him,
—one word from your lips will be life or
death to the poor youth."

This appeal of her thoughtless attendant, on the very point which was then
agitating and absorbing all Angelica's
thoughts, only added a keener edge to
the painful sense of her position. She
trembled at the thought that a fellow-
creature's life—perhaps his salvation—
was involved in the consequences of the
advice she might give him.

But though she appeared not to heed
what Arghyrousa said, those words—"one
word from your lips will be life or death
to the poor youth"—vibrated with intense
distinctness along every fibre of her heart.
She felt oppressed by that kind of mental

nightmare under which there is a vivid consciousness of wretchedness, without the power of giving outward expression to the terror it produces.

As she remained silent, Arghyrousa continued her observations in an undertone which was neither soliloquy nor dialogue,—

" Kyr Nikóla may not fare quite so well, peradventure. Those Klephts are punctual enough when they promise mischief. They may think it less trouble to chop off a head than to slice off a pair of ears or a nose. But Kismet rules everything in this world ; and there is many a Christian who would bear such a misfortune of his neighbour's like a true Mussulman. I am sure if I had such a husband, I would——"

Angelica here interrupted Arghyrousa, in a tone in which the deep dejection of her spirit overcame the anger she might otherwise have expressed at such language, however unmeant to reach her ears,—

"Arghyrousa, do not, I beseech you, distress me by such light talk. Were you Kyr Nikóla's wife you would act as she is bound to do. I am very unhappy. I want your counsel, and not your foolish jests."

Arghyrousa, so gently and touchingly rebuked, said—"Dearest mistress, I would not grieve you for all the jewels on the Sultan's turban. Forgive me for thinking aloud; but after all, a woman is not blind, though she be a wife; and I declare that if my Christodhoulo were to treat me as——"

Angelica put her hand on Arghyrousa's mouth, and said—"If a wife has her eyes open to the faults of her husband, it must be only for the purpose of guarding him against the evil consequences of them."

This conjugal morality was a cut above Arghyrousa's mark; but she respected her mistress's feelings; and while she wondered at her superfeminine forbearance, internally completed her unfinished phrase, —

"Were Christodhoulo to treat me as certain husbands treat their wives, I would not stir a finger to save his ears, no, nor yet his neck, from the knife of the Klephts."

While poor Angelica is revolving in her anxious mind all the possible consequences of the fatal task imposed upon her by Alỳ Pasha, we must follow the latter to his hall of audience in the Garden Palace, whither he had previously given orders that Mehemet Effendi should be conducted, on his return from his mission to Rapsistas.

CHAPTER XXXVI.

BEFORE the Citizen Plenipo is ushered into the presence of the Albanian autocrat, we must turn back, meet him half way on his route from Rapsistas to the capital, and try to gather from the conversation which passed between him and his now boon companion, Papa Jerôme, what was really and truly the object of his mission. The *chasse-café* which the Reverend Effendi had indulged in, had so effectually chased from his bewildered brain all traces of his former self, that, were a man capable of metaphysical speculations under such circumstances, he might have entertained rational doubts of his identity. After he was with some difficulty hoisted into his saddle by the joint assistance of the Surejee and the

Tatàr, he broke forth into a rhapsody,
compounded of reminiscences of his early
studies in the Propaganda, and scraps of
bacchanalian poetry in the drunken strains
of the Bard of Shiraz :—

" Arise, O cupbearer ! give the full cup.
Scatter dust on the head of Care. Although vile be our name in the estimation
of dull sages, what care we for disgrace or
renown ?" . . . "*Mesci, mesci* . . . *Bicchier
di vino* . . ."

To these effusions, the sense of which
bid defiance to all the decencies of Moslem
sobriety, as the dolorous tone in which
they were uttered violated all the laws
of harmony, Bouchon responded by shout-
ing out the *Marseillaise* and *ça ira*,
with a *sans-culotte* phrenzy, inspired by
maraschino and patriotism, that elicited
from the old Tatàr, who was busied lighting his tchibouk, no notice but a grave
shake of the head and exclamation —
" *Ahi giddy Delhi Elchì !*—Oh, the jolly,
mad ambassador ! "

However, it is in the nature of all sublunary joys to be evanescent. — The more vivid the flash of that momentary lightning, the deeper the gloom of the succeeding darkness.

As the party approached the term of their journey, and the light of the mishal burning in the great court of the seraï began to be perceptible by the gleam shot up into the dusk, which had now blended all objects in one common hue, the thought that he must in a short time be standing before his redoubtable master to report his proceedings, suddenly finding an entrance into the Effendi's confused brain, sobered him, and at the same moment filled him with dismay at the consciousness of his having not only totally neglected his master's injunctions, but of having actually fraternized with one who, it was only reasonable to suspect, was little better than a spy.

The truth must be told. Titus Bouchon was indeed no better. The relations subsisting between the Sublime

Ottoman Porte, and the still sublimer French Republic, at the period we are telling of, were rather of a sickly hue. The two powers, since the landing of the French army in Egypt, were no longer at peace; but war had not yet been actually declared. The French Embassy had not yet been accommodated with lodgings in the Seven Towers, at the expense of the Sultan.

It was the dream of the French Commandant in the Ionian Islands, recently delivered over to the Republic, at the fall of the decrepit government of Venice, that he could cajole his neighbour of Epirus into fraternizing with the great nation. Why, indeed, might not the good old Turkish system, reducing, as it then did, all ranks to the same level by a common oppression, fraternize with the modern democratic autocracy, which practically sacrifices individual freedom at the shrine of an impossible social equality? The difference is only in the name.*

* *Vide* Note.

Well, then, Bouchon was by the same Commandant selected to try the experiment of fraternization on the crafty Toshki. The *spécialité* which recommended him for the task was his supposed knowledge of the foreign languages, a branch of learning in which the French, from the patriotic conviction they then cherished that their own was the universal language of civilization, did not at the time excel. Bouchon knew that *nix* stood for *rien;* that *come stà* was equivalent to *comment va-t-il?* that *selamalek* meant *bon jour; ti diavolo* was *que diantre;* and finally, he believed in the dictum of Beaumarchais as to the fundamental basis of the English language. He had picked up, besides, a few of the phrases common in the Levant, composed of Spanish, Arabic, Italian, and other dialects which form the mosaic called *lingua Franca;* these, eked out with his own native French, and uttered with that imperturbable self-complacency which imposes not more on the ignorance of others than on a man's self, left no doubt in his own mind that he was equal to the mission which was now entrusted to him. Perhaps he was not aware, that the principal reasons which weighed with his chiefs was that he was one of those bustling, troublesome fellows, the loss of whom would not be deplored. If he succeeded in getting the information required—well; if not, why he might be disavowed, and, if hung for his pains, there was no great harm done. Bouchon, therefore, had no written instructions the seizure of which could compromise his employers; and this giving free scope to the shifts of his own ingenuity, suited his adventurous *gamin* spirit the better, as it left him at liberty to assume any airs his vanity might prompt.

By the time the travellers had crossed the trench, and passed the ragged palisades which marked the boundary of the Albanian capital on that side, and the jaded horses were beginning to stumble against the rough pavement of the straggling street which led to the rendezvous; the Frenchman, gradually awakening to a sense of his plenipotential responsibilities, and casting about to gather together his wits, which his jollification had caused to stray far and wide, was accosted by Mehemet Effendi, who rode up to the side of his horse, and said,—

"Monsieur du Bouchon, we are now nearly arrived at our journey's end; and I shall presently have to report to the Vezir my master, in obedience to his Highness's commands, the purport of your mission. You must be sensible that your admission to his Highness's presence depends upon the satisfaction which I can give him on that point. The Vezir will doubtless require the exhibition of the credentials which authorize you to speak to his Highness on behalf of your chief; it may prevent delay, and save trouble, if you will give them to me, to lay at the feet of my master the Vezir."

"Que diable! quelle mouche a piqué le vieux bonhomme!" said Bouchon with the tongue of his inner thoughts, as he listened to this semi-official harangue, spoken in a tone of husky gravity, which formed a ludicrous contrast with the recent merriment.

The Frenchman perceiving the *changement de décoration*, instantly got upon the stilts of his dignity of *Citoyen Français*, and replied, while he gave an emphatic thump to the tricolored cockade stuck on his hat: "Voilà mes seules lettres de créance. — Si votre maître refuse d'y ajouter foi, tant pis pour lui."

It is astonishing what a vision of future woes is shadowed forth in a swaggering *" tant pis pour lui ! "* There is no saying how often it has served to help many an impudent *fanfaron* like our friend Bouchon out of a difficulty.

"Le seul titre de Citoyen Français est une garantie suffisante de ma loyauté. Votre Pasha fera comme il voudra. Pour moi, Tite Bouchon, je saurai faire respecter l'honneur de la grande nation. C'est à lui seul que je déclarerai l'objet de ma mission." Then followed another vigorous thump on the cockade.

The poor Effendi was dumbfounded at this unexpected somerset of his dear friend Tite Bouchon, on his high ropes. What could he say to the Vezir? and, between the autocracy of the one and the republican insolence of the other — what could he expect but hard knocks from both?

But he had not been initiated in the wiles of Jesuitism for nothing, and so he made up his mind to a system of interpretation, which should not commit himself with the Vezir.

After passing through a variety of dark narrow lanes, which led away from the centre of the town to the skirts of it, on

the side opposite to that by which they
had entered, the party at length emerged
into a broader space, and rode into the
court of the same seraï, where the wretched
Effendi had so lately been rated by the
sable portion of his harem. The lively
reminiscence of that scene suggested by
the spot did not contribute to soothe his
anxiety, or give him courage at the anticipation of the interview now about to take
place.

He had hardly time to dismount from
his steed, before one of the Vezir's attendants came to hasten him into his Highness's presence.

"The Vezir has been expecting you this
half-hour," said the man, in a tone which
sounded to the poor renegado's ears like
the echo of his lord's impatience, and the
forerunner of any thing but a gracious
reception. The message completing the
process of sobriezation restored him to
his senses, and to his native pusillanimity.
He followed the Tschaoòsh into the

dreaded presence, trembling with terror at the apprehension of the result of the coming conference

After a few minutes, the same Tschaoòsh came and summoned the Frenchman, who with a swaggering gait and creaking boots, soiled with the dust of the road and the sweat of his jaded horse, followed him, and was about to pass from the open gallery into the hall of audience, when he was arrested at the door by another attendant, who, by words which Bouchon's polyglotism did not compass, gave him to understand, by an unmistakable gesture, that he must pull off his boots before he proceeded further. The papouches left at the outside of the door testified to the existence of the custom which he was called on to practise. Now, although Bouchon professed the principles of Sans-culottism in the abstract, he was in no humour to carry out those principles to the abstraction of his boots. He, there-fore, instead of attending to the hint, was pushing his way through the perdèh into the Vezir's presence, when he was forcibly pulled back by the Tschaoòsh; and as he resisted with violent struggles to disengage himself from the Turk's grasp, his spurs coming entangled with the long drapery, he fell, and, in his fall, brought down the official to the floor. The other attendants, meanwhile, coming to their comrade's assistance, succeeded in divesting the refractory Frenchman of one of his boots.

The noise of the scuffle, and the delay occasioned by it, having excited at once both the impatience and the curiosity of the Vezir, he sent Mehemet Effendi out to ascertain the cause of the unusual scandal.

On his report to the Vezir of the incident which had occurred, his Highness, who had made up his mind to treat the diplomat in his own style, ordered the Effendi to go out again, to express his regret at the indignity which had been offered *his Excellency,* in consequence of the ignorance of his people. The Elchi was at liberty to approach the Pasha with his boots on, and would, it was hoped, forgive the too-zealous punctilio of men who were unacquainted with the peculiarities of Frengui manners.

Bouchon, soothed by this civility, which he attributed to the dread of the French power and to respect for his own personal dignity, drew on his boot, adjusted his dress, somewhat discomposed by the scuffle, and strutted into the room with all the importance of a real Plenipo.

Without waiting for an invitation, he went and seated himself familiarly on the divan, near the Pasha, who, apparently taking no notice of the *liberté-égalité* style of the citizen's manner, turned to the Effendi, who stood in an humble attitude in the middle of the floor, and said,—

" The Elchi Bey has no doubt his letters of credence from his government. Before we enter into conversation on the object of this unexpected visit, I desire to have them read to me. Let the Elchì deliver them to you."

This very reasonable request having been duly turned into the best diplomatic French that the Italian Effendi could muster on the occasion, was a puzzler for his extempore Excellency, Tite Bouchon. Credentials he had none to deliver—nor any instructions, as the reader has already been informed, beyond the general caution to have his wits about him, to observe everything, to ascertain the dispositions of the Vezir towards the Republic one and indivisible, and to uphold in every circumstance the dignity and sovereignty of the Grande Nation — *quand même* — an expression which gave the Citoyen, in his capacity of one-thirty-three-millionth fraction of that sovereignty, *carte blanche* to be as insolent or impertinent in the assertion of the French pretensions as he thought proper.

Of this the *gamin*, whose native presumption was further heightened by the pot-valiance derived from his late libations of maraschino, of which he was yet redolent, with a partial mixture of the perfume of the weed, was quite ready to avail himself. The apology which had been made by the Vezir for the forcible abstraction of his boots, and which he interpreted into a dread of the French name, only constituted an additional stimulus to the development of his ambassadorial arrogance. And so the Sieur Tite assumed at once the language and manner of a Roman Pro-Consul towards a subject kingling dependent on the nod of the S.P.Q.R., as such a character might be represented on a minor theatre in the banlieue of Paris.

"Vous pouvez répondre au Pasha qu'on ne demande pas aux délégués de la République Française des lettres de créance. Leur parole d'honneur suffit. Appuyé sur cette cocarde glorieuse," pointing to the

enormous three-coloured pen-wiper on his
hat. "Un Citoyen Français est reçu par-
tout où il se présente comme représentant
de la Grande Nation. C'est là son droit
—je le reclame ce droit, moi, Tite Bouchon, au nom de la République."

Nothing of the tone, gesture, or look of
" *Moi, Tite Bouchon,*" while he uncorked
himself of this stream of his *grande nation*
impertinence, escaped the watchful eyes
and ears of Alỳ, who, not having implicit
confidence in the fidelity of his renegado
Dragoman, trusted more to his own observation than to the words uttered, for the
judgment he was to form of the *quo animo*
of the pseudo-Elchì.

The nervous hesitation which Mehemet
Effendi evidently betrayed, while stam-
mering out a few unmeaning words to
serve as a decent envelope to the Frenchman's rudeness, confirmed the Vezir in his
surmise that Citoyen Bouchon's mission
was all a sham, or, to use the Oriental phrase
we have adopted from themselves, "*Bosh.*"

He anticipated the Effendi's interpretation by observing, in a dry, sarcastic tone, "I see how it is; he has no letters of credence. He is no Elchi; and the sooner he lets me know what he really is, and what he is come about, the better. Tell him so, without circumlocution."

Papa Jeróme knew, from the peremptory tone and the scowl of the eye with which this order was given, that he might as well cut out his tongue as dare to evade it. He repeated the Vezir's words to Bouchon, and added—"Son Altesse dans ces occasions ne badine pas."

"It is a sport," observes Bacon, "to see when a bold fellow is out of countenance, for that puts his face into a most shrunken and wooden posture."

Such was the posture of our friend Bouchon's face when he found himself thus stripped by the four pithy words—"*He is no Elchi*"—of the protection which the Law of Nations, even the most barbarous, accords to the character of foreign envoy.

The self-appointed delegate of the Grande Nation, finding that the threatening tone of the bully would not do, fell at once down to the flattest level of the sneak. His volubility and presence of mind abandoned him altogether, and he remained silent and abashed, casting an anxious look towards the perdèh, which he expected every moment to see drawn aside to make room for the entrance of the executioner.

Whoever has observed the motions of a hard-hearted, practised old tom-cat, as he watches a miserable mouse, after inflicting the first squeeze of the inexorable claw as a prelude to the lingering agony which awaits the poor, trembling, wee beastie, may judge of the sport it was to the Pasha to watch the alarm of the detected cheat.

Alỳ had not quite made up his mind how he should deal with him, whether to hang him as a spy, *in terrorem*, or to turn him to account in some other way, when he perceived galloping into the court an express Tatàr, who, throwing himself off his horse, hurried up-stairs, and, without waiting to be announced, came and delivered at once, into the Vezir's own hands, the despatch with which he was charged.

After a glance at the superscription, the Vezir motioned with his hand to a sinister-looking fellow, whose head just then was seen thrusting itself from behind the folds of the perdèh. It was the same with whom the luckless Frenchman had had the wrestling-match in the corridor. The man immediately stepped forward; and, kneeling at the side of his master, received his commands whispered in his ear, which he immediately hurried forth to execute, letting drop a glance, half-ferocious, half-contemptuous, on poor Bouchon, who, combining in his terrified mind the ominous motion of the master's hand with the truculent look of the man, gave himself up for lost, surmising no less than that he was doomed to die the

inglorious death of a spy. His consternation was made manifest by the sudden
whiteness of his face, the more conspicuous from the black frame of moustache and favourites in which it was set,
and by the sweat which burst forth on his
forehead.

Alỳ, affecting not to perceive this,
turned with ironical courtesy towards the
wretched man, while he said to Mehemet
Effendi,—

" I beg the Elchì Bey to excuse me
while I read my despatches. I have given
orders for his disposal till I have leisure
to hear what business brought him to
Ioánnina. Do you entertain the Beyzadé,*
meanwhile."

So saying, the Pasha clapped his hands,
the usual attendants came in, and the
disaccredited diplomat and his entertainer
were unceremoniously thrust into an adjoining waiting-room, where, as he entered
and surveyed what he shudderingly fancied

* *Vide* Note.

might prove the destined place of his execution, Bouchon had cause enough to address to himself the rebuke which many an improvident adventurer has lamentingly uttered, but too late,—

" *Que diable avais-je à faire dans cette galère ?* "

CHAPTER XXXVII.

CITIZEN Leonidas Tite Bouchon's meditations as he sat for some time opposite
to Mehemet Effendi, with no light but
that of a small iron lamp hooked against
the wall, were anything but entertaining.
The subjects his mind dwelt upon belonged to what, in the learned discussions
of the Académie des Sciences, would be
ranged under the head of Comparative
Pathology. His excited fancy, assisted by
the recollection of some desultory reading
of the registers of the Inquisition, and of
scenes he had heard described by one
who had endured a temporary captivity
in the prisons of the Dey of Algiers, passed
in review the various sensations of a living
being experimented upon by a Turkish
Magendie, under the process of impale-

ment, strangulation, roasting *à petit feu,*
or decapitation with a blunt yatagan.
The conclusion he came to, as to which
of these various modes of making his exit
off the stage of life he should prefer,
supposing he had the option, was a
decided repugnance to them all.

" Dis donc, Papa Jerôme Effendi, ça
coûte-t-il bien cher de se faire Turc?"

With this home question Bouchon
abruptly broke the silence in which he
remained plunged for full ten minutes
after his dismissal from Alỳ Pasha's
presence.

To this question, which seemed to re-
vive some disagreeable reminiscences in
the Jesuit's mind, the latter replied by
one of those distortions of the facial
muscles, and the upheaving of the shoulders, which supply the purpose of speech
with the gesticulating natives of Southern
Europe, and may be interpreted according
to the imagination of the observer.
Bouchon, without asking for a meaning,

or waiting for a more distinct reply, said
with an effort, as of one working himself
up to a heroic resolution,—

"Enfin, c'est égal—coûte qu'il coûte,
je me fais Turc. Un honnête homme
se doit tout entier à l'humanité — tous
les hommes sont frères—et je ne res-
terai pas moins bon français quoique je
porte un turban au lieu d'un chapeau.
Crois-tu, mon bon Effendi," continued he,
in a less desponding tone, at the hope of
escaping from the horrors he had been
pondering over, " crois-tu que le Pasha
refusera de me prendre à son service, si
je me fais Turc?"

The renegado, delighted at the chance
of having a companion to keep him in
countenance in his degradation, responded
with alacrity,—

" *Au contraire,* the Pasha is too happy
to secure the services of Frenguis, and you
can't do better than propose yourself to
him. But in what capacity do you offer
yourself? Do you know anything of

gunnery?—The Vezir has been some time looking out for some one to manage his foundry of cannon at Bounila.—Do you know how to cast guns? Can you make gunpowder?"

"To be sure I can," said Bouchon. "Was not I manipulator to those *savans* at Cairo? Did not I assist in unswathing that mummy? Did not I nearly blow up the laboratory in assisting at one of their famous chemical experiments? *Parbleu!*"

There was nothing in any of the departments of science or of art that Bouchon was not ready to undertake, so he might escape the horrid fate which his fancy, during that ten minutes' silence, had pictured to him.

Presently the noise of steps and bustle of people passing to and fro in the adjoining gallery was heard, when, the door being unlocked, the sinister-looking Tschaoòsh entered, bearing his staff of office, and addressing himself to Mehemet Effendi, told him that the Vezir's orders were to conduct the Elchì Bey into his presence with all due honours ; finishing the delivery of his message, which was performed with decorous gravity, with—

" *Bouyouroun, Efendim.*"

Poor Bouchon's knowledge of the Turkish tongue was too slender to comprehend a syllable of what was spoken. He was so brain-bound by the apprehensions which haunted him, that all he could do was to mistake the word *Bouyouroun* for *Bourreau.* His fears instantly interpreted it into an invitation to come out and put himself *en rapport* with that formidable personage, whom he fully expected to find standing outside, with the bowstring or the yatagan all ready for business.

Before the Effendi had time to do his office of interpreter, the terrified Frenchman repeated in agony,— "Je me fais Turc ! je me fais Turc ! Je crois au citoyen Mahomet. Je ferai tout ce que Monsieur le Pasha voudra de·moi."

While Papa Jerôme is explaining to his
terrified friend Bouchon the gracious purport of the message, which, to say the
truth, had as much perplexed him as its
misapprehension had scared the poor
Plenipo, we must account for the sudden
change in the Vezir's line of conduct
towards him.

During the short interval which has
elapsed since Alỳ Pasha dismissed this
interesting individual from his presence,
a change has come, not over his spirit, but
over his schemes for carrying into effect
the suggestions of that crafty spirit.

The despatches delivered in such
haste brought him intelligence of the
movements of the French forces at Corfù,
which, in proportion as they excited his
alarm and distracted him with doubts as
to the ultimate intentions of his ambitious
neighbours, made him feel more than
ever the absence of his agent, Yanko,
through whom alone he could hope to
obtain authentic information by means

of his secret relations with Corfù, which should enable him to make effectual preparations for the defence of his territory.

He now began seriously to apprehend, that the Klephts would be as good as their word, and that should he longer delay satisfying the condition they insisted upon, of his restoring Photo Tzavella to liberty, he would be deprived for ever of the services of his indispensable confidant.

In his perplexity Alỳ determined, according to his laudable custom, to try the arts of dissimulation, where he could not obtain by more direct means the object of his desires.

It was in this state of mind that he gave orders that the Frenchman should be reconducted into his presence with the ceremonial observed towards a real Elchì.

The shifting of the scene was so sudden and unexpected, that when poor Bouchon, who had been struggling under a waking nightmare of bowstrings, and

yatagans, and impaling stakes, found himself actually seated beside the Pasha, with
his own head on his shoulders, and courteously presented with a cup of pure Moka
in a cup ensconced in an elaborate fila-
gree saucer, and jessamine pipe three
yards long, with an amber mouthpiece
studded with rubies, the change had
nearly crazed him, and he could with
difficulty persuade himself that he was
not acting a part in a melodrame at the
Porte St. Martin. How he got there
was more than his poor bewildered brain
could then make out. He was still more
confirmed in the belief that he must be
somebody else than himself, when Mehemet Effendi interpreted in grave, official, diplomatic-sounding language, the
speech which he was ordered to address
to *His Excellency* on the part of His
Highness the Vezir, Alỳ Pasha of Tricala
and Ioànnina, in the following terms : —

"Monsieur l'Ambassadeur,—His Highness the Vezir commands me to express,

in the first place, his deep regret at the misunderstanding which for a moment arose with respect to your official character and the object of your mission. The intelligence he has just received has cleared up everything to his entire satisfaction, and His Highness is now ready and desirous to attend without further delay to the important confidential communication which he understands that your Government, justly relying on your discretion and intimate knowledge of the great interests at stake between the Sublime Porte and the illustrious French Directory, have entrusted to Your Excellency."

Christopher Sly was not more astonished when, waking from his drunkenness, he was accosted with "Will't please your Lordship drink a cup of sack?" than was our Sans-Culotte at finding himself all of a sudden dubbed an Excellency, and invited to a dish of confidential politics with a Pasha of three tails.

" *Le diable m'emporte si j'y entends*

goutte," bethought within himself this ambassador *malgré lui*, as he listened, wondering, to the unexpected compliment bestowed on his discretion and diplomatic knowledge.

But what was the confidential communication which he was charged with? What did he, Tite Bouchon, know of the relations between the Sublime Porte and the illustrious French Directory?

N'importe, c'est égal.

Unlike the drunken tinker, he, drunk with his own self-conceit, instead of deprecating the honour, greedily gorged the bait presented to his vanity by the crafty Albanian, and sending out from his pipe a self-complacent puff of smoke, assumed at once a consequential air and attitude, which seemed to say, " Upon my life, I am, after all, an ambassador indeed!"

Under this persuasion he, in the lack of instructions beyond those he had received, " to have his wits about him, and to fraternise with the natives," gave him-

self full powers to pour forth a rhapsody
of nonsense, made up of the high-sound-
ing phrases which in those days teemed
in all the proclamations and state-papers
of " La Grande Nation" about the Rights
of Man, Liberty and Equality, Sans-Culottism, Social Regeneration, the Reign
of Reason, Sovereignty of the People,
&c. &c.

The poor Jesuit Dragoman broke out
into a profuse perspiration in despair at
the task assigned him of translating, or,
as the German phrase is, *oversetting*
the Frenchman's jargon into intelligible
Turkish.

The interpretation, such as it was, only
served to confirm the suspicion which
Alỳ had entertained from the first, that
Bouchon was no better than a forlorn
spy, and a very ill-chosen one. However,
as he had not quite made up his mind
whether it were worth his while, or the
expense of a rope, to hang up *His Excellency*, the Pasha affected to listen with

the most deferential gravity to Bouchon's gibberish, as if it really meant something serious.

In the reply which he directed Mehemet Effendi to make, he expressed an earnest desire to secure the protection of the French commander at Corfù in the scheme which he pretended to entertain, of throwing off his allegiance to the Sultan, and placing himself under the vassalage of the French Government. His admiration of the new French *régime* was, he affirmed, heightened by what he saw of the manners produced by it, as exemplified in the dignified bearing of the Elchi Bey himself; and he finished by throwing out a hint of his disposition to adopt the revolutionary costume, and the philosophic creed of *La Carmagnole* and *ça ira.*

Bouchon swallowed all with the characteristic gullibility of a Parisian *badaud,* and eagerly accepted the Vezir's commission to convey to the French General an invitation to hold a conference with him at some convenient place on the coast opposite Corfù, where they might settle the terms of the agreement he was anxious to come to with the French authorities.

"To-morrow morning," said Alỳ, "your Excellency shall have an escort for your journey back. In the meantime, should anything more occur to me to be communicated to you before your departure, Mehemet Effendi, who has my entire confidence, shall wait upon you with my final instructions."

The Pasha, then calling to him his chibookchee, who stood at the end of the room, preparing to hand the farewell pipe to the Elchì Bey, ordered him to go bid the Tschaoòsh in waiting to be at hand to conduct His Excellency to the conak assigned him, and having deposited him there, to proceed to the Bishop of Arta's, and summon his Panïerotes to the Great Seraï, there to await the Vezir's arrival.

This important conference being now

happily terminated, to the no small satisfaction of the improvisated ambassador
and his interpreter, Alỳ waved his hand
with a gracious smile as Tite Bouchon
turned to take his leave, — a ceremony
which he, remembering what he had
learnt of Oriental manners as represented
on the stage, performed with such extraordinary gesticulations and grimaces, that
he had hardly got out of hearing before
the Pasha gave vent to his contempt for
the Guiaoor, by shaking the collar of his
benish, and exclaiming,—

"'Αναθεμαῖο μάσκαρὰ — The wretched
buffoon ! Τὸν ἐγέλασα ὅμως — Have I not
humbugged him ?"

Bouchon was, on his side, equally satisfied with his own cleverness in having
paid off the Turk in the same coin, and,
instead of losing his own head, as he
might have done, having got a pasha of
three tails *dans sa poche*, as the foreign
phrase is, when one Diplomat flatters him-

self he has *bagged*—*i.e.* duped—his brother Dip in some negotiation.

He was roused from this delectable state of self-gratulation by the rush of the Pasha's attendants, who, as soon as he emerged into the gallery, each stretched out his hand, accompanied by that ominous dissyllable which grates upon the Frengui's ear the instant he sets foot in any part of the Sultan's dominions, — *Bakshish.* There is not an echo in Turkey that does not naturally respond " Bakshish " to any word pronounced by a Frengui traveller.

Our *gamin*, whose vanity interpreted every word and gesture as an homage paid to his ambassadorial dignity, took it for granted that these worthy individuals sought the honour of *une poignée de main* of His Excellency, out of sheer disinterested respect for his person; and as he was just then benevolently disposed to adopt the condescending line, he did not hesitate to gratify their desire, and gave to each his hand. Turkish officials, however, are not, more than others of their class, content to be put off with such empty pay, and the chibookchees, and cafédgees, and all the host of other *jees*, repeated with still great importunity the cry of " Bakshish, — bakshish ! "

" Que veulent-ils donc avec leurs pois chiches ? " said Bouchon, appealing to Mehemet Effendi, who accompanied him to the head of the stairs.

" La buona mano, ou pour-boire," replied the Effendi.

" Allons donc, à quoi bon un pour boire pour des gens qui ne boivent que de l'eau ? Allez, mes amis, allez à la fontaine. Vous y trouverez de quoi humecter vos pois chiches. Allez. Pour moi, je ne donne rien pour rien."

So saying, he pushed the Turks aside ; and calling out to his conductor, who was busy lighting a lantern, " En avant, marche," he would have proceeded on

the way to his night's lodging, when he
was stopped at the exit of the court by
the Surejee, who, standing by his horses,
assailed him with the same ominous cry
of "Bakshish."

"Comment diantre! encore des pois
chiches!" exclaimed the persecuted Plenipo, who was on the point of vindicating
his dignity and defending his pockets by
a blow; when the cautious Padre Effendi,
who watched his progress, and apprehended the coming mischief, called out
to the Surejee that the Vezir paid for the
Elchì Bey.

"A beggarly Guiaoor of an Elchì must
he be, indeed, that can't pay a bakshish
for himself!" muttered the Surejee, as he
mounted his horse and rode out of the
court, leading his jaded cattle to the
menzil. "Let me only catch the infidel
dog on the road to-morrow, and if I
don't get a bakshish out of him I'll cut
his ears off!"

Bouchon, unconscious of the fate impending over those *organs* (to use an expression consecrated by the example of the great American novelist), followed the lantern-bearing Tschaoòsh through long, tortuous, narrow lanes, which led to a wider street, where stood a house of better appearance and larger dimensions than the rest.

" Here we are at Kyr Yanko's," said the Tschaoòsh ; and he gave a great thump on the door with his staff.

A pause ensued : but no answer being returned, the thump was repeated ; and, this time, not without effect, for the noise having roused from their slumbers a pack of mangy curs, the scavengers of the quarter, whose nightly bivouac was established on a neighbouring heap of filth, they struck up a symphony in every note of canine music, which was presently responded to by a rival pack of mongrels in the next street.

The nerves of Citoyen Bouchon, already excited by the events of the day, and the

want of repose, were not proof against the
irritation of such canine discord. He
drew his sword, and rushed upon the yelp-
ing, barking brutes. He had better have
let them alone, for he soon had to defend
himself against the assault of the whole.
pack in front, rear, and flanks; and might
have shared the fate of Actæon but for a
lucky thrust, which, maiming one of his
assailants, diverted, as is the habit of that
degraded race, the fury of the rest upon
their disabled colleague.

Meanwhile, in proportion as the patience
of the Tschaoòsh began to ebb, his
thumps went on increasing in venom,
accompanied by certain adjurations peculiar to Moslem spite, which reflect in very
uncivil terms on the ancestors and kindred
of the offending individual. But the more
he repeated his knockings, the less notice
seemed to be taken of them, till he came
to the conclusion that the house was
empty.

Upon which he quietly turned to the

hapless Frenchman, who, fatigued with the day's work, had seated himself on a block of stone near the door, and was beginning to nod with sleep, said—"*Dour, Bakalum*—Wait a bit; we shall see."

Then, without further ceremony, leaving Bouchon *planté là* in the dark, he proceeded to the Bishop of Arta's house, to deliver the Vezir's summons to attend forthwith at the Great Seraï.

CHAPTER XXXVIII.

AMID the surprise and hurried confusion occasioned by the sudden fall of Photo's jailer, every one was too much occupied with thoughts for his own safety, not knowing who next might be struck down, to heed what became of the intended victim. Photo exhausted by his emotions, and dragged to the ground by the fall of his baffled executioner, was hardly conscious of his escape from the stroke of the knife which but the moment before he had seen uplifted against his throat. Well might he fancy he was dreaming when he heard close to his ear, in a suppressed voice, as of one who feared to be heard— "Photo, my child, have courage ; it is I, Samuel: fear not. I am at hand, but take no notice now."

The Dervish had hardly time to breathe these words in the poor boy's ear, before the old Buluk Bashi, with two other of the Vezir's Palikaria, approached, and he withdrew himself from observation, that he might be more at liberty to watch the issue of the event.

They raised the boy from the ground, and supported him with a greater degree of tenderness than he had been accustomed to be treated. Samuel followed them with his eye, as they conveyed him by some rough steps cut in the rock down to the edge of the lake, where a boat was waiting in which the prisoner and his escort were embarked, and which presently was seen rowing across the water to the islet in the middle of the lake, about half-a-mile from the promontory on which stood the seraï.

It was after ascertaining this fact that Samuel resolved on the bold step which was described in a preceding chapter, the result of which is now to be explained.

Towards the close of that same day, as

the shadow of the western mountains were stretching over the plain of Ioánnina, and involving the town, the seraï, and the waters in one misty hue, there landed from a small skiff on the island the gaunt, wild figure of the Dervish, who presented himself to the Buluk Bashi seated on a low stool near the shore.

Not far from where he sat was a building which had once been a Greek monastery, since converted by Alỳ Pasha to the uses of a prison, for the incarceration of the unhappy beings who fell under his displeasure. It was here that Photo was now confined.

As the Dervish walked towards the old soldier, the latter saluted him gravely with " *Selam Aleïkim,*" which was returned with equal gravity by the holy man, by " *Aleïkim selam.*"

The latter having taken his seat, the Buluk Bashi offered him his tchibouk, but the Dervish declined it.

"Why, Babàm!" said the old soldier,

"'t is not yet Ramazan; and if it were, the sun is not gone down."

"I am under a vow," said the Dervish, with great solemnity, meant to impress the soldier with an idea of his Moslem rigour.

"That must be a serious vow," observed the Buluk Bashi, "which forbids you tasting such prime tabak as this: 't is genuine Latakié. It was a bakshish from Mukhtar Pasha, for the service rendered him when I secured this wolf's cub the other day at the Bishop's house.

"It is concerning that same wolf's cub that I am come here. He has laughed at all our beards,—a scandal to our faith not to be borne. He must be made to eat his own filth, and I have vowed to the Vezir that he shall.

"Here, look at this (and he drew out of his bosom a paper, which he put into the Buluk Bashi's hand), and you'll see what we have to do with him."

The old man read the paper, and ex-

amined with great attention the impression
of the Vezir's signet.   As he folded it up
carefully, and placed it securely within the
folds of his own garment,—

"I understand," said he: "'t is my
warrant for conveying this son of a thief
to the Hammam over the water.   Well,
you may wash him clean and change his
rags for a new suit, but you might as well
think of turning a blackamoor white as to
bend the obstinate temper of this wild ass's
colt.   I saw enough of him when he first
appeared before the Lalà, and afterwards
when I took him at the Bishop's, and again
this morning when the knife was at his
throat.   'T is a pity he's not a Moslem,
for, after all, Guiaoor though he be, he's
as brave as a young lion.   But we must
obey the Vezir's command, and get over
the lake before nightfall.   Do you, Bahàm,
go in and rouse him, while I call the
caïkjee to bring the boat round.   Your
skiff won't hold us all; and here, give the
poor wretch this crust: we feed dogs

rather than they should starve under our eyes."

Samuel had some difficulty not to betray his emotion at the gruff kindness of the old Turk, which had brought him the very opportunity he had been so anxiously watching for, to see and speak to Photo without inconvenient witnesses.

"Where is he?" said he, with affected indifference.

"There. Draw back that bolt; now push open the door, go down the steps, and when you are at the bottom you'll find him at the end of the passage on your left. There is not much light, to be sure, but enough for the time you'll be there."

So instructed, the pretended Dervish groped his way down into a subterranean vault, which was originally the crypt of the chapel belonging to the monastery in earlier times.

Before he could distinguish any object by the dubious light which struggled for an entrance into the dark and dank vault through a narrow opening or loop-hole in the massive wall, the sound of one breathing heavily, as in a disturbed sleep, directed Samuel's attention to a recess in the vault, in which he presently descried the form of the poor weary prisoner on the broken pavement. The attitude in which he there lay indicated exhaustion, and the prostration of all strength. It seemed to be that of one who had let himself drop down at a venture ; the attitude of utter despondency. Except that the sound of breathing gave evidence of life, the form over which Samuel stooped with unutterable compassion, was that of one whose spirit had escaped beyond the world of sense.

"Poor boy!" exclaimed the Papàs, forgetting for a moment his assumed character of a fanatical Dervish, as he raised Photo's wan, yet still beauteous face to the light. It was smeared with the blood of his executioner, and his long flowing locks were clotted with it—so was his tattered shirt. The echo of his own voice repeated by the arched vault, re-called Samuel to thoughts of caution, and to the necessity of silence.

The movement caused Photo to open his eyes, and as they fell on the Dervish's cap and dress, a confused recollection of the look which had been fixed upon him during the morning scene, mingling with that of the sound of the voice he had heard, and with all the hurry of the scene through which he had passed since the morning; he still remained as in a dream, unable to distinguish between the phantasms of his own bewildered brain and the reality of things. But when the same words were whispered into his ear, which had been constantly vibrating along the nerves of his heart, as if in mockery of his woe,—

"It is I, Samuel; fear not;" the sudden conviction that it was no longer an illusion, but that the voice was indeed at last

that of a friend, darting down into his
inmost soul, produced the effect of an
electric shock upon his whole frame. The
poor, weak, half-dead creature sprang
upon his feet, and, throwing his arm
round the neck of the old man, burst into
a flood of tears, and wept aloud. "My
father!—my father!" were the only words
he could utter in the first agony of
feeling.

Samuel pressed the poor lad to his
heart with all the affection of a father;
his stern nature would have melted by
contagion into tears, but that he remembered the necessity of dissembling.

"Be calm, Photakimou," said he in a
low tone. "Thou must for a while dissemble as I do. Thy life depends on thy
prudence. While we are in presence of
others, I know thee only as a vile Guiaoor;
and thou must forget that I am thy friend.
Watch all my movements as if thou didst
dread my enmity, as I am on the watch
for the means of thy escape. For this am

I come, or to die.with thee, if I cannot for thee."

He was here interrupted by the tread of the Buluk Bashi, as he descended the steps leading to the vault, and called out to the Dervish that the boat was ready.

On this, Samuel reassumed a rough, savage tone, in speaking to Photo :— "Come, move, you infidel whelp!—move up!" But before they emerged into daylight from the subterranean darkness, and could be exposed to the observation of the old Turk, Samuel, as he supported the tottering steps of Photo, stiff with the long confinement of the manacles in which his limbs had been pinched, contrived to give him information and counsel for his guidance in the new and unexpected emergency in which he was about to be placed.

When the pretended Dervish, followed by his victim, emerged from the subterranean darkness into daylight, which was now fast giving way before the lengthening shadows, he found himself in presence of three other Palikaria, attendants, or orderlies of the old Buluk Bashi, who were completely armed with musket, sword, and pistols, intended as an escort charged with the secure conveyance of the prisoner across the water.

When the whole party, consisting of the Buluk Bashi, the three Palikaria, the Dervish, and Photo were stowed away in the boat, the old fisherman, in shoving her off from the rock, and at the same time stepping upon her gunwale, caused her to heel over so much that one of the brave fellows, who, like the rest of the Skypetars, had the same dread of the water as is attributed to the Czar Peter, drew his pistol from his girdle, and swore with a great oath that he would shoot the caïkjee if he did not keep the boat quiet.

The old fellow took the threat very coolly, and seemed to enjoy the Palikari's alarm, which was evidently shared by his companions, except the old Buluk Bashi, who had seated himself very comfortably in the bottom of the boat, and was most unconcernedly lighting his pipe. Instead of being solicitous to diminish their alarm, the skipper observed,—

" The boat is a crazy one, and not over roomy. There is a monoxylon at hand, if there is anybody to row it,—perhaps it might be safer if this were lightened. Hallo! Moré Spiraki, bring the other oar, and run down here. You are lighter, and more active than your old uncle; you shall row the Effendis across, and I'll get into the monoxylon with one,—perhaps the Dervish Aga will have no objection ?"

To this the Dervish gave his assent, and the new arrangement being made to the satisfaction of the hydrophobic Pali-karia, the larger boat pushed off first, rowed by Spiraki; and then the Der-vish, being seated at the bottom of the monoxylon, serving as ballast, the old Charon, standing up and using a long

pole, or boat - hook, also pushed off,
but so leisurely that Samuel, fearful of
losing sight of his charge, in his impatience gave vent to it by a Greek oath:
for which he could have bit out his
tongue, and tried to hush it up by an ex-
plosion of right Turkish anathemas accompanied by Moslem abuse of the slowness
of the boatman.

The daylight that still lingered after
the sun was set was not yet so dim but
that Samuel could perceive the significant
smile and twinkle of the eye of the old
fisherman, as he calmly listened to him,
without apparently heeding the objurga-
tion, or in the slightest degree accelerat-
ing his motion.

"Do you think, Moré Papàs, that I
don't know you? Hold," said he, with
deliberate indifference, as he perceived
the discovered Papàs attempting to rise
and grapple with him; "don't betray
yourself, and so defeat your own purpose. Fear me not,—I, too, am a faith-

ful man, and you may want such an one
to help you ere long to save that poor
child yonder. Did not I contrive to get
you apart just now from his jailers, to let
you know that I and my boat, and my
nephew there, are heart and soul at your
service ? Now, knock me down if you
choose ; but remember," added he, laughing, " you can't do so before I have pitched
you into the water : and a pretty pickle
you would be in, up to your neck in mud,
with a rope of weeds round your legs.
But now, only trust an honest Christian
and we'll sink or swim together."

There is a freemasonry between honest,
earnest minds, by which they become instinctively known to each other. Samuel
at once trusted the good old fisherman.

" Thank God !" exclaimed he, " I have
found what I prayed for—help in the
moment of need. But how didst thou
know me ?"

" Oh, as for that," said the fisherman,
" thy speech betrayed thee. There's

nobody blurts out an anathema with such
venom as a Papàs when taken unawares.
But there is no time to lose in idle talk.
We are nearing the landing-place, and
must be agreed upon the plan of operations for effecting the escape of this poor
boy."

By the time the sun was down the boats
touched the land, at a spot near to which
a narrow lane led to a neighbouring hammam, or public bath, to which Photo was
conducted under the guard of the Buluk
Bashi and the sham Dervish, followed
by the Palikaria, while the old boatman
and Spiraki, having joined company, the
former informed his nephew of what had
been arranged between him and Samuel,
the result of which will be unfolded in the
sequel of this tale.

CHAPTER XXXIX.

As

"Satan now is wiser than of yore,
And tempts by making rich, not making poor,"

so Alỳ, acting upon the suggestion of the
Dervish, abandoned for a while the system of terror, and resolved to assail his
victim by the seductions of voluptuous-
ness. It was with this purpose that he
gave the order for Photo's removal from
the dungeon to the bath, on his emersion
from which he was made to exchange his
tattered prison garments for a new suit
of the graceful Albanian dress, than which
none is better calculated to set off to the
best advantage the person of a handsome youth, such as the young Suliote was
by all beholders allowed to be. At the
same time Alỳ issued his directions that
an entertainment, a grand *ziafet*, should

be prepared in the great hall of audience, on the effect of which in awakening the dormant passions he relied for debauching and laying prostrate, in the dust and filth of sensual excess, the virtue of the inexperienced young mountaineer.

Music, dancing-girls, buffoons, a magic lantern, all the paraphernalia of an orgie suited to the abject taste of believers in a sensual paradise, the description of which no writer can attempt, and no reader can listen to, without abhorrence and disgust, were summoned for the occasion.

In further pursuance of his satanic scheme, the worthy disciple of the arch-tempter determined to bring Angelica and Photo together, reckoning that the virtue of both would give way before the peril of the alternative which he had recently proposed to Yanko's wife. How little does the worldly-wise profligate know of the hidden sources of strength in the uncorrupt heart!

The superintendant of the harem, the

old lady already introduced to the reader, received the special instructions of Alỳ with respect to the arrangements for the meeting, which he directed was to take place at nightfall in the pavilion on the lake.

This pavilion, or summer kiosk, was a spacious room detached from the mass of the buildings occupied by the harem, at the extremity of the rocky promontory that jutted out into the lake.

Built upon piles, and slightly raised above the water's level, and open to the east and north, it afforded at the close of a sultry day a delicious coolness, the sensation of which was heightened by the sound of the plashing of a fountain placed in the centre of the marble floor, and by the fragrance of an abundance of flowers arranged in vases on the edge of the basin which received the water of the fountain.

The three sides of the kiosk which overhung the lake were occupied, in the Turkish style, with a divan or sofa, backed

by cushions embroidered in gold and silk
of the most costly workmanship, and by
their luxurious softness inviting to that
dolcissimo far niente — the attraction and
bane of all sunny southern climes.

A long covered passage or gallery, from
which there was an outlet by a side-
door upon a wooden platform, serving as
a landing-place from the lake, formed
the only communication between the pavilion and the women's apartments above,
which were reached by a flight of stairs
at the other end of the passage. Mid-
way there was a door, which, when closed,
prevented the communication between the
harem and the pavilion.

It was to this place that Angelica was
conducted after the Pasha had left her.

The ostentatious deference with which
she still continued to be treated by the
old mistress of the robes, following so
immediately upon Alÿ's insulting language and behaviour, only confirmed her
worst suspicions of all that was plotting

against her. Her suspicions arose to alarm, when, looking round, she no longer saw Arghyrousa at her side, but, instead, encountered the scrutinizing eye of the ancient duenna fixed on hers with the leer of a she-satyr.

"*Korkmà janèm*,—Fear not, my darling," said she; "don't look so sad: there's some one coming here presently I know your soul is longing for, who will keep you company and cheer you up till it is time for the *ziafet* to begin—such a *ziafet* as you have never seen, even in a dream, with those beautiful eyes of yours.

As she spake, she was for chucking Angelica familiarly under the chin, but Angelica shrunk from the touch of the odious creature in unmistakable disgust.

"Well, well," continued the hag, "pout as you may now, and give yourself airs, as young things do; you'll change your note before to-morrow morning. One piece of advice I'll give you, my sweetheart, and that is, not to give yourself

such airs with our lord the Vezir, or
mayhap your bed may be there;" and she
pointed with her finger downwards to the
lake—"you know what happened to Kyrà
Phrosyne."

So saying, she left the pavilion.

It was a relief to Angelica to be rid
of so odious a presence; but the continued absence of Arghyrousa filled her
with present anxiety, so great as to make
her heedless of the threat implied in the
parting words of the mistress of the
revels.

The thought came across her that her
sharp-witted maid had, perhaps, been
stripped of her idiot mask, convicted of
intellect, and either turned out of the
seraï, or thrown into the lake; and with
that thought came the sickening feeling
of hopelessness expressed by the inscription over the infernal gate—"*Lasciate
ogni speranza voi ch' entrate.*"

The sun had now set. The glow of
the heavens where he sank was reflected

against the eastern sky, which gleamed
with a momentary radiance that was repeated by the waters of the lake, and,
mingling with the slowly-increasing light
of the risen moon, threw a dim, silvery
ray into the pavilion, whence Angelica
fancied she could just discover, amid the
darkening horizon, the peak that overhung the ravine of Kalarýtes.

Thither she turned her anxious eye,
with an inward regret at having quitted
the shelter of her obscure home, which
was only allayed by the consciousness of
having done so in the fulfilment of an
unavoidable duty. As she kept gazing
upwards, the stillness of the heavens, out
of whose dark, tranquil depths silently
emerged, one by one, the multitude of
stars, insensibly imparted a soothing influence to her wearied spirit, bringing
with it the ineffable solace felt by all believing hearts in the contemplation of
those divine attributes of exquisite tenderness and illimitable power, so touchingly

exemplified in the simple words of the
greatest of poets:—

" He healeth those that are broken in
heart; and giveth medicine to heal their
sickness. He telleth the number of the
stars, and calleth them all by their
names."

Angelica was aroused from the reverie
into which the soothing calmness of the
scene had thrown her, by the sudden
entrance of some one into the pavilion.

As she looked round, eagerly expecting
to see her faithful Arghyrousa, she discovered, standing within the perdèh, the
figure of one whose dress, as far as she
could distinguish it in the dubious light,
was that of one of the Vezir's pages.

It was Photo. He advanced with a slow
and uncertain step into the centre of
the hall, and the moonlight, which now
streamed in at the open casement, falling
upon his delicate features, emaciated by
long suffering, imparted to them a marble-
like paleness, which to Angelica, whose

last and transient sight of them was asso-
ciated with the idea of death, gave him
the spectral appearance as of one risen
from the dead.

She gazed on the apparition without
being able to utter a word. Her pure,
guileless spirit, was stirred to its inmost
depths by a thousand conflicting emotions. Her heart was hot within her.
She yearned to tell Photo how deeply
she sympathised with his desolateness.
But the bitter sneer of Alỳ which haunted
her memory—" 'Tis that handsome youth
you care for, and not your vile husband,"
kept her speechless.

Then, across the confusion of her
thoughts, came the Vezir's parting words :
" If the boy perishes, his blood and thine
own be on thy head, thou wife of Yanko."
They now echoed, like the voice of a fiend
suggesting evil fancies, which distressed
Angelica's innocent mind with an agitation almost like that of remorse.

She remained silent, and motionless as a statue.

Photo hesitated for a moment. He then advanced a step nearer, and said :—

" It is I,—Photo. Do you not know me, Angelica?" Then, as if he had presumed too much, he added,—" Pardon me, lady; the place in which we meet ought to remind me that you must have forgotten the Suliote captive."

The reproach conveyed in these words, and the tone in which they were spoken, were too much for poor Angelica's overwrought feelings.

" Oh, Photo ! Photo !" was all she could say, as she held out her hand to him, and burst into an agony of tears.

Photo now ventured to approach Angelica. He fell upon his knees, and taking her hand kissed it, and pressed it to his throbbing temples, and held it there as if to allay the bewilderment of his brain.

" You did not use to call me *lady* when

you were sick at Kalarýtes—I was your sister, then," said she, as, bending over him, her tears trickled upon Photo's fore-head. "Why such bitter words now? Am I not here an unwilling captive as well as you, Photaki? and," she added, with hesitation, "did I not run these risks with the hope that the redemption of my husband would save your life, too?"

"Oh, Angelica," exclaimed Photo;—"sister, may I call thee again?—forgive the rash words of a poor death-stricken wretch like me. But am I not now in a dream? Art thou, indeed, the same who watched me so tenderly in my weakness, and called me brother? or am I with the angels in Paradise? If it be not all a vision, let me hear again that voice of sweet pity, and then let them strike the blow I have so longed for in vain."

Arghyrousa, who had entered the room unperceived by her mistress, and till now had remained silent, with a watchful eye upon the door near which she stood as sentinel, here suddenly interposed,—

" There's no time for dreaming or seeing visions. Realities will soon be upon us. Say quickly what you have to say."

" Arghyrousa is right," said Angelica, addressing herself to Photo ; "I must be brief. Know then, Photo, that your life depends on the answer which you return to the Vezir's proposal which he has commissioned me to make to you. He simply requires that you accept his pay, and enter his service as one of his Palikaria. There is no more question of your renouncing your Christian faith. What answer——"

" Stop!" said Photo, with a fierceness which strangely contrasted with the desponding tenderness of his manner till then. "Am I really in a dream? Did you consent—you, lady, with Hellenic blood in your veins—to be the channel of such a proposal from this blood-drinker to me, a

Suliote? ˉ He—the vile oppressor of our country, he *simply* requires that I, a child of Suli, accept *his* pay,—eat bread offered by his bloody hands? Surely," and he grasped Angelica's hand with convulsive energy, "surely, Angelica, you did not ask my life as a favour from the bloody .Turk, and on *such* conditions?"

Then, as if ashamed of his violence, he let go Angelica's hand, and turned away from her in deep dejection of spirit.

"Thou noble youth!" exclaimed Angelica, catching inspiration from his honest anger. "Oh! that thou wert, indeed, my brother! Such was my loved Sotiri. No, Photo, no. Think not such hard thoughts of me. The Turk imagined that I should urge you to accept his proposal, and made my life as well as yours depend upon my success in persuading you. But God in heaven is my witness that I would die a thousand deaths sooner than breathe a word to make you falter in the resolution I know was in your heart, or to save myself by such base counsel. You think better things of your sister now, don't you?" said Angelica, as she looked into his eyes, where she saw a tear glistening in the bright moonlight.

"Oh, Angelica! What hast thou said? And must *thou* perish, too, if I refuse? Surely to save such a life, I might——"

"Hold!" cried Angelica, and she put her hand upon his lips. "Tempt not thyself and me to falter in the path of duty. God will rescue us both from this peril, if He will——but if not, if we are to perish, let us die unsullied by a single wavering of purpose."

Photo felt the rebuke conveyed so gently in these courageous words, which strung anew his determination, that, for one instant only, seemed to be giving way before the fear of involving Angelica in his fate.

"God's blessing on thy manly heart!" exclaimed he, as he pressed Angelica's hand to his own heart, and then kissed it with the passionate fervour of a martyr, no longer holding back, but eager to rush into the flames. "Thy sweet voice is to my ears like the sound of the trumpet to the warrior. Lead me, thou guardian angel, where thou wilt—thou canst lead only to glory."

At this moment steps were heard approaching along the passage, and presently a black face, partially lighted by a lantern held up by the owner, was indistinctly seen, like the moon in an eclipse, protruding itself from behind the door-curtain, and then a hand thrust forward whose finger pointed towards Photo, while an inarticulate sound came gurgling through the thick lips of the harem mute.

" 'Tis a summons for Photo," whispered Arghyrousa. "The Vezir must be returned sooner than he intended. There's no help for it. He must go. But don't be afraid. Only, Photo, take a simpleton's advice. *Dissemble* a while; it will give time for counsel, and for the rescue which is at hand."

The mute now advanced into the room, and, holding the lantern up to Photo's face, seized him by the hand, while he held back to cast one last look at Angelica.

" Bear thee bravely, my brother," said she. " Have no thought for me — but trust in God. Happen what will, our home is there;" and she lifted up her hand to heaven.

" The thought of thee and of thy words, my sister, shall make me braver than a lion," said Photo, as the black mute, now grown impatient, led him away.

" When you have to deal with a fox," observed Arghyrousa, after their departure, " you must pay him trick for trick. 'Tis all quite right to be as innocent as doves, but there's no harm in using the wisdom of the serpent; and so, dearest mistress, pray put on this ragged cloak and veil of mine, with these old boots, and be ready to slip into the boat that will soon be here to carry you away,

There are people coming and going about this feast which is preparing for you. You'll not be taken notice of in the crowd. The attendants of the harem are all busy at the other end, with that horrid old woman at their head; and if any of them were to see you, they will only take you for stupid me, and say ' *El' humd 'ul illah !*' at getting rid of such rubbish. That dear old mad-cap, Dervish Caloyero, has contrived it all—you may trust to him to get you out of any scrape. And here he comes—listen—don't you hear the splash of the oar ? Here, quick, sweet mistress mine, wrap the cloak round you, draw the veil close over your face. So. There's the boat already at the landing-place. I see him. 'Tis Papàs Samuel himself."

Arghyrousa peeped into the passage — "There's nobody there—the middle door is closed, the door on the lake is a-jar. Come along, come, and God go with you, dearest Kyrà."

Angelica hesitated. "But, my Arghy-rousa, you are coming, too. I won't go without you. I can't leave you behind. I can't consent to save myself at your expense."

"Never mind me," said the faithful creature; "my going with you would spoil all: there's no room for us two in that crazy boat. Go you must. Don't be like Lot's wife. Worse things than death await you, if you linger in this foul den. If I told you all I have seen and heard within the last hour——But there's no time. Go; for Heaven's sake, go."

Angelica shuddered at the dreadful hint. The horrors it suggested to her mind overcame all further hesitation. She embraced Arghyrousa in silence, and the two loving women parted from each other, not knowing when or whether they should ever meet again.

Arghyrousa listened till the sound of the boat, as it glided into the moonlight mist towards the further end of the lake, died away upon her ears. Then, after all the excitement of the day, finding herself alone with no more to do, but wait what should come next, she sat herself down, and gave way to the emotions which, for the sake of her mistress, she had kept under control, as long as there was anything to be done in her service, and indulged in the luxury of an abundant flood of tears.

CHAPTER XL.

THE Bishop of Arta, in obedience to the summons delivered to him by the Vezir's Tschaoòsh, immediately proceeded to the seraï, accompanied by his palikari Yorgaki, who, as the Bishop alighted from his mule, put into his master's hands a packet, which he said an unknown man had thrown into the court as they were leaving the house, and then disappeared.

Ignatios, who was accustomed to receivē many petitions and letters of the kind, was about to thrust it into his bosom, when, glancing at the superscription by the blaze of the mishal which was burning before the entrance of the seraï, he was surprised to find that the packet—none of the cleanest—was directed simply to Alỳ Pasha, without any of the titles of honour, courtesy, or respect usual in addressing the dignitaries of his rank in Turkey.

The haste with which he was ordered into the presence of the Vezir the moment his arrival was announced, gave Ignatios sufficient intimation that the business he had been sent for was of no ordinary importance.

The Bishop was no sooner introduced than Alỳ bid him, by a motion of the hand, take his seat on the divan, and at the same time ordered all the attendants, who were standing at the other end of the room, to leave it.

Alỳ remained for a while apparently absorbed in thoughts which he seemed to be trying to disentangle, while he kept passing his fingers like a comb through his thick beard, the silence being only interrupted by the bubbling of the water in the crystal narguilé, as he occasionally inhaled the smoke of the fragrant weed.

"I sent for you, Kyr Dhespotés," said

he at last, " to consult you on affairs of great importance to the Devlet. I know I can confide in your discretion, your experience, and your integrity. I know you to be a good man, a dutiful rayàh of our master the Sultan, and that your study is to promote his Highness's service, and the good of all men."

Ignatios acknowledged the compliment by a modest inclination of the head, while he thought within himself what was coming next. Were not these honied words the prelude to some griping avania to be imposed on his people, or to some painful sacrifice to be required of himself?

The Pasha proceeded,—

" News have reached me this evening which trouble my soul. Those Frenches who have turned the world upside down are now our near neighbours. They are not satisfied with having invaded Egypt, but they want to possess themselves of these coasts, and are preparing troops and all manner of warlike stores for that purpose. It is my duty, as a servant of the Devlet, to oppose their schemes; but I am at a loss for a trusty agent to assist in obtaining accurate information of what these satellites of Antichrist are about at Corfù. Do you know, Dhespota, of any man that could be safely employed in such a service?"

The Bishop guessed that Alỳ was feeling his way to the mention of Nikóla Yanko's name, who, as everybody knew, was the Vezir's *âme damnée* in all matters of espionage or detective police in the neighbouring islands; but he replied, as if he knew nothing of such matters,—

" *Ypsilotate*—May it please your Highness, I am not conversant in these affairs— I am no politician. The fishermen and traders of the coast opposite, who have dealings with the islands, are more likely to assist in getting news of the movements of the French ships and troops."

"Yes," said Alỳ, after a pause, during which he appeared to be musing on the suggestion of Ignatios; "I should be in no difficulty if Yanko were here; but he is, unfortunately, in the clutches of those cursed Klephts."

He was silent again for some moments, and then continued, in a still more dulcet tone,—

"A thought has just come into my head. Could not you, Bishop, undertake to negotiate his ransom? Lawless and untamed as these Klephts are, your name and office, and, most of all, the reputation of your virtue, is not without its influence among them; and such conditions as I am willing to offer, proposed to them under your guarantee, would, doubtless, be gladly accepted by them. You would thus be rendering a service, not to me only, but to the government, to say nothing of saving the life of a fellow-creature."

This parenthetical tenderness for the life of a fellow-creature, in the mouth of the man of blood, did not particularly edify the good Bishop. He was not so simple but that he understood the Pasha's proposal to signify, in dry, unbuttered language,—"Be so good, my Lord Bishop, as to redeem my rascal's head at the risk of your own."

Now, it must be confessed that Ignatios, kind, disinterested, charitable as he was on all occasions demanding the exercise of those episcopal attributes, felt no particular alacrity to jump at the proposal.

Instead of returning a direct answer to it, he withdrew from his bosom the packet given him by Yorgaki, and placed it on the sofa between himself and the Vezir.

"This," said he, "may perhaps enable your Highness to judge what are the conditions on which the detainers of Kyr Nikóla's person are disposed to give him up. Till those conditions are known, the offer of a guarantee for their fulfilment would be premature."

" *Bakalum!* " said Alỳ; "what is this? where does it come from? "

The Bishop having explained how he came by it, the Vezir unfolded the packet, and disclosed to view a pair of human ears of uncommon dimensions, which appeared, from their freshness, to have been subtracted from their native block not many hours before.

They were fastened together by a twine of silk passed through a hole bored in each of them. The end of the twine was secured to the paper in which the ears were wrapped up by a seal of soft yellow wax, bearing the impression of a Greek cross.

As Alỳ took up the paper to read the uncouth-looking manuscript which he perceived to be scrawled thereon, in a strange-coloured ink, the ears dangled against his fingers, wide and flat, like a Lord Chancellor's seal appended to some unintelligible parchment.

The meaning of the writing was clear enough. It ran thus :—

"The head to which these ears belong will be sent after them, if the Suliote, Photo Tzavella, is not landed, alive and unhurt, before Ascension Eve, at the Krýonerò, under Macrinoro. These and no more."

This notice was corroborated by a postscript in the well-known handwriting of the late proprietor of the enclosures referred to :—

"I, Nikóla Yanko, certify that the above-mentioned are my own ears, and for the sake of the Panayïa, St. Basil, and all the saints, do thou supplicate the Vezir, our master, on thy bended knees, to save the head of his faithful slave, thy unhappy husband, and quick."

Alỳ read the paper with no other change of countenance than a lurid twinkle of his cruel grey eye, which spoke of the revenge he hoped some day to take upon the pen-

man of the impertinent note of his comrades.

"Yes," said he, addressing himself to
Ignatios, in a tone of indifference, which
was meant to disguise his mortification at
the insolence of these bandits, thus beard-
ing him in his own territory; "there's no
need to certify to those ears — anybody
could tell them to be Nicolaki's among a
thousand pairs."

And he handed over the paper to the
Bishop, who, good man! would willingly
have dispensed with the honour of such
a confidence, and felt an internal shivering as he took the paper, and felt the cold
flesh strike against his disabled hand, as
he held up the writing to the light with
the other.

Alỳ smiled at the Bishop's embarrassment, as, having finished the perusal of
the Klephtic document, he sought where
to deposit it.

"Kyr Dhespota," he said, "you are

not so used to these things as I, who have to keep these lawless Klephts in order."

He then, with his diamond-hilted dagger, which he drew from his girdle, stuck the point of it into the Yanko cutlets, and tossed them out of the window, near which he sat. The dogs beneath—the *habitués* of the palace-yard—were presently heard fighting and worrying one another in contention for the dainty morsel.

Alỳ looked again at the writing, and asked the Bishop on what day was the festival of the Ascension.

" The day after to-morrow, Ypsilotate; to-morrow evening is Ascension Eve."

" There's no time to be lost, then," observed Alỳ, with an anxiety which he now no longer sought to conceal. " I must get that man out of the hands of those Klephts at all hazards. The Sultan's service must go before everything."

Ignatios felt that the critical moment of the young Suliote was arrived; he held

his breath,-waiting in the utmost anxiety
for the Vezir's next words.

"Dhespota," continued he, "'t is plain
that those lawless vagabonds will not release my servant, except in exchange for
that Klephtopoulo.   But how convey him
to the rendezvous in time? and who will
answer for his not escaping on the way,
and   afterwards   for   the   delivery   of
Yanko?"

"If your Highness will be pleased to
employ my poor services in this behalf,"
said Ignatios, "I will undertake to effect
the exchange.   Trust the lad to me, and
I will answer for *him*, at least."

The Pasha's eye here shot out a glance
at the Bishop, in which suspicion of the
reverend man's sincerity, and contempt of
his credulous *bonhommie*, were strangely
blended.

"I may trust *you*, Dhespota," observed
he; "but what security have you for having
it in your power to fulfil such an engagement?   For, mark me, if you *do* engage

yourself in this affair, I shall exact its fulfilment to the utmost, or——"

The good Bishop, nothing alarmed by the threat implied in the unfinished sentence, intent only upon the work of mercy he had at heart, and upheld by the consciousness of his own singleheartedness, calmly replied,—

"I willingly incur any risk or penalty you may impose on me, but I have no security whatever to offer but my own faith in the word of the lad."

"How?" said Alý, in a tone which marked his utter incredulity. "The *word* of that thief's cub! And pray, where, when have you communicated with him? *What* word has he spoken?"

"None at all," calmly replied Ignatios, who did not fail to mark the suspicion implied in the last question. "My meaning simply is, that upon the child's pledging me his word to whatever I may require of him, I will be answerable to your Highness with my head for the release of

Kyr Nikóla into my hands, if not already too late; or, in default, for the return of Lambro Tzavella's son into yours."

"Well," observed Alỳ, "I have heard it quoted from your vangeel that faith can move mountains, but I would sooner trust to Mount Mitzkel's coming over to this side of the lake than to the Suliote's putting himself again into my power." And here he chuckled outright with undisguised self-complacency at this his own *naïve* admission of what a dangerous customer he was to deal with. "'Tis not in the nature of man that it should be so," continued he. "If that is your only security, Dhespota, 'tis good for nothing. But I will supply you with a sure one. I accept your services upon the condition you have offered. Your Holiness I can trust, and so will I the Klephtopoulo under guards and manacles. But there is no time to lose. You must be on the road at the instant. I will give orders at once to ——"

Before the Vezir had time to complete his sentence, he was suddenly interrupted by a great scuffling, which was heard going on in the adjoining ante-chamber, and the sound of angry voices, the cause of which was presently revealed by the violent pushing aside of the perdèh, and the inrushing of young Photo, with his arm uplifted as if prepared to repeat the blow which, from the excited appearance of his whole person, the distortion of his nostrils, the gleaming of his eyes, it was readily surmised he had been inflicting on some adversary with triumphant effect. He was without the richly embroidered upper garment which distinguished the Vezir's pages. His long dark hair was flung back in wild disorder, like the mane of a young lion, just coming out all chafed and ruffled from his first skirmish with a host of " small deer."

Heedless of the Vezir's presence, Photo's eye, still glittering with wrath, no sooner met the calm yet anxious look of his friend than at once his arm dropped, and with a hurried step across the room he went and with bended knee put the hem of the Bishop's robe to his lips and forehead, and then retiring a few steps stood in a submissive posture before him.

"How now, insolent!" exclaimed Alỳ, incensed by this unceremonious intrusion, and still more by the young Suliote's disregard, not to say contempt, of *His Highness's* presence, contrasted with such marked deference to the *Rayàh* Bishop; and he clutched a pistol which hung on the wall near him.

Ignatios immediately rose from his seat and placed himself between the Vezir and the boy.

"Forgive him, O Vezir!" he cried; "the poor child is ignorant, and beside himself with all which has befallen him to-day. Pardon the fears of——"

"Fears!" interrupted Photo, with a shriek, in which scorn and anger were strangely blended.

"Oh, my father," added he, with an accent of almost penitent supplication, which singularly contrasted with that shriek, "attempt not to save my life by such excuses. You have taught me to fear God only. It was not I that began; they," (pointing to the next room,) "*they* mocked me, because of these new clothes—they told me I was no more a brave Suliote; but one of *them*, and that I was glad to change my rags for these embroidered jackets, and all because I was afraid to die. Could I hear such mockings and lies, and not resent it?" And then, baring his right arm up to the shoulder, as if making ready for another fight, his eyes glistened with exultation at the sweet revenge he had taken. For, in truth, the scuffle which had preceded his recent apparition before the astonished Pasha, caused by the impertinent remarks of His Highness's pages, had terminated in their discomfiture before the fury of the young mountaineer. The self-sufficient coxcombs had not calculated how the energy of a noble spirit, sharpened by the unmerited taunts of base natures, can make up, on a spur, for lack of physical power.

Alỳ Pasha, never losing sight of the urgency of the more important business he had in hand, dissembled his resentment, and affecting to laugh at the boyish quarrel, and to disapprove of the impertinence of his menials, he clapped his hands, and to the attendant who instantly appeared from behind the perdèh said aloud :—" Tell the Tschaoòsh Bashi to put those three young blackguards in prison; to have them well fed with sticks (*i. e.* to be bastinadoed) till I give orders for a change of diet. And, hark ye, let the Tatàr Agassi come here directly."

"Now, Dhespota, proceed we to the conclusion of this business. Be seated."

Photo, at a glance from the Bishop, was now about to leave the room, but Alỳ called him back. "Do thou remain here, my child," said he, in an almost paternal tone; (the old hypocrite!) "thou art a party in this business of ours."

"You said, Dhespota, that you would take on yourself to effect the ransom of Yanko, by the exchange of this lad against him."

Ignatios bowed assent to the truth of the Pasha's assertion, and Photo's attention to the dialogue became rivetted.

Alỳ P. "You engaged, moreover, if Yanko were not forthcoming alive, to deliver *him*" (and he moved his head with a significant look towards Photo) "back into my hands."

Photo, who now understood that he was indeed a party, and that a principal one, in this business, felt his heart beat thick with irrepressible anxiety, as he caught the cat-like side-glance of the Vezir's eye, and waited for the Bishop's answer.

Bishop. "Yes, O Vezir! I did so; and I now repeat, that if your Highness will entrust the lad to my keeping, for the purpose of being exchanged against Kyr

Nikóla Yanko, I engage, on the forfeit of
my head, to effect the exchange ; or, failing
therein, to bring back the boy, and deliver
him back into your own hands."

Alÿ P. "Dost thou hear, Photo, what
it is the Dhespotés engages for thee?"

You might have heard the poor boy's
heart knock against his ribs.   His colour
went and came, the sweat stood upon his
brow, betraying the quivering of his soul,
as it caught a glimpse through the mists
of the future of his possible return to his
hated prison, after the one remaining
present chance of escape from it.

Alÿ Pasha fixed his cruel eye upon him,
waiting his answer.

Photo faintly said, " 'Ηχουσα,—I have
heard."

The Vezir turned from him with a
scornful toss of his head, and continued in
a tone of triumphant incredulity to the
Bishop,—

"Well, Kyr Dhespotés, you see now
what security you have for fulfilling your

engagement. Are you so credulous, or so little acquainted with the character of these Klephts, as to trust them? Trust *me*, there is no security but fetters and a well-loaded pistol."

Ignatios had marked the agitation of the poor boy, and had no difficulty in guessing what was the cause of it. "O Vezir," said he, and at the same time he encouraged Photo by one of those looks of deep sympathy which carry comfort and strength to the fainting spirit; "there be stronger fetters than those made of iron. Nothing so binding as the chains of gratitude and love. To these alone I trust for my security and success in the accomplishment of your Highness's business."

Photo greedily drank in the Bishop's words, of which the full *personal* import was understood and assented to by his young undepraved heart, and the moist glistening of his expressive eyes, as he looked with reverent affection on his friend's calm and dignified countenance, and ratified beforehand his acquiescence in the engagement made by Ignatios on his behalf.

" Say, my child," continued the Bishop, " art thou willing to abide by the promise thou hast heard me make to the Vezir on thy behalf?"

Photo eagerly answered, "O Dhespota, whatsoever thou bid'st me do, I will obey to the letter."

" Hear me out, and then speak, boy. If the Vezir commits you to my charge, and that it should happen that Yanko be no more, or that in any way his release be prevented, wilt thou promise to come back with me? 'Tis on this I pledge my head to the Vezir——"

" Say no more, O Dhespota! my father," replied Photo: " to save a hair of thy head from harm, I will endure anything. But one condition only I require; having given *you* my word, I will submit to no other constraint to keep me to it."

"You talked of fetters and pistols, O Pasha!" said he, now boldly turning to the man who by a nod could deprive him at the instant of life or liberty. "Bind me, force me, and I hold myself free from the promise I have made to the Bishop. A free Suliote's word is as true as his sword. Treat me as a slave, and I will be as false as all slaves are."

The Vezir listened as one who hears a foreign language, of which he tries to guess the meaning. Great thoughts come from the heart—noble sentiments can be understood only by noble hearts—the mere intellect takes no cognizance of them but as of metaphysical abstractions.

Alỳ pondered a while without uttering a word. At length, as if roused from a reverie, in which he was occupied weighing the risks for and against the step, suddenly he addressed the Bishop, saying, "Be it so, then. But there is no time to be lost. You must depart instantly. Go and prepare for your journey. Remember, Dhespota, you are answerable for the return of Yanko or of that boy."

As Ignatios rose to take his leave, the Vezir added, " Remember our bargain : Nicolaki or that boy — or ——"

The rest of the phrase was interrupted by the entrance of a Tatàr, all ready equipped for a journey, whom Alỳ addressed in the hearing of the Bishop,—

" Emin Aga, you will accompany the Bishop to Salahora ; take care that His Holiness wants for nothing on the road."

" *Bash ustum,* — Upon my head, I will answer for the Bishop's safety," - replied, obsequiously, Emin Aga. " I will go and see that all's ready ; " and he was leaving the room, when a motion of the Vezir's hand called him back, and bending low to kiss the hem of his master's garment, the messenger remained in that attitude while this injunction was whispered in his ear,—

"If that Klephtopoulo go out of the road, to the right or left, shoot him at once."

CHAPTER XLI.

I⟨T⟩ was the Eve of the Ascension. The sun had set in unusual splendour beneath the purple wave of the Ionian Sea, flinging upward to the sky a sheaf of golden rays, as if to strew with light the path of some celestial messenger across the wilderness of gorgeous clouds heaped in dark, towering masses, high above the distant horizon. It seemed as if preparation were making in the heavens for the celebration of the crowning festival of that faith by which mortal man, degraded by sin below the level of the beasts, is raised above the dignity of angels.

But there was one wretched being to whom that glorious spectacle brought only despair. Yanko had now been four days in the hands of the Klephts, who, imme-

diately after the despatch of Samuel to
Ioánnina, had consulted their own safety,
endangered by their too close proximity
to that capital, by carrying off their captive to the more distant and secure retreat
afforded by the jungles of Macrinoro, at
the eastern extremity of the Ambracian
Gulf.

Yanko, erst the sleek, well-fed, com-
fortable Proëstòs of Kalarýtes, now ex-
tenuated with hunger and anxiety, unwashed, unshaved, without his ears—the
loss of which he was unpleasantly re-
minded of by the shrill trumpet-notes of
legions of demon musquitos that sought a
settlement on the vacant places—sat all
that day, alone and silent, in the prison
assigned him by his captors, expecting the
required ransom.

The prison was a cave on the slope of
the mountain, the mouth of which faced
the setting sun, and overlooked the waters
of the gulf and the islands beyond.

From that height the practised eye

might distinguish or divine many a classic
spot among the lands which stretched
from the shores of the gulf far away, on
the right into Epirus, and on the left into
Acarnania and Ætolia.   With the aid of
fancy's telescope, it might, perhaps, dis-
cern amid the waters connecting the Ambracian Gulf with the Ionian Sea, that
narrow pool, once crimsoned with the
mingled blood, and crowded with the contending galleys of all the nations, when
the empire of the world was awarded to
the Victor of Actium.

But the prospect brought no such visions before the dull eye of Yanko. What
were the historic agonies of the thousands
who perished, centuries since, in those
waves—what were the fortunes of Au-
gustus, or Antony, or even of the beauteous Cleopatra, to that unhappy wretch,
tortured with the apprehension of losing
his head in a few hours more, by the same
operation which had so recently deprived
him of his ears ?

As Yanko sat and watched the declining orb, his heart kept sinking with it; and when he perceived the last sparkle of light suddenly quenched in the sea-wave, the groan which burst from him betrayed the terrors of his soul. The fated hour was come, but no ransom appeared.

The twilight, prolonged by the bright glow reflected from the western sky, was quickly succeeded by the shades of night, which were deepened by the impending masses of the mountain, made darker still by the thick forest which clothed its sides from the summit to its sea-washed base.

Before the entrance of Yanko's prison-cave there stood a huge, uncouth splinter of grey, weather-beaten rock, like the vedette of an advanced patrol on the look-out for an approaching foe. On the level space which formed a natural terrace at the foot of this rock, and between it and the cavern's mouth, a fire was lighted, round which the Klephts now began to assemble, while Yanko sat motionless, anxiously listening to every sound, in gloomy anticipation of the fate which that gathering portended.

An unconcerned spectator might have found much to admire and to interest him in the countenances, gestures, and attitudes of these Hellenic Robin Hoods, as the red glare of the fire flashed upon their picturesque figures, and their dark shadows were projected in every fantastic shape against the sides of the cavern and the trunks of the surrounding trees. In this band, or *Klephtourià*, consisting of about forty (which seems to be the orthodox number for thieves, bandits, conspirators, *et hoc genus omne*), there was hardly one who would not have been eagerly admitted into the artist's studio, to serve as a model of manly symmetry and beauty. Such, doubtless, were the living men, whose human forms divine have been transmitted to us in those exquisite sculptures — monuments of the imperishable glory of Grecian art — which still breathe and move along the lines of the Panathenaic procession of the Parthenon. Such were they, too, who strove for the chaplet of parsley or laurel—the corruptible crown which rewarded the victor in the gymnastic struggles of the Olympic games, in the presence of the assembled nation. These, indeed, appeared in a costume less encumbered with drapery, yet not more picturesquely heroic than the Greek Palikari, with his short white kilt of many plaits, his embroidered velvet vest, his silver greaves, scarlet leggings, and light sandals.

But there was in the expression of the countenance and look of every one of these outlaws, however handsome or delicately chiselled might be his features, something which marked the lawless, reckless life of violence to which they become habituated who maintain a constant struggle against systematic oppression. The bold and cruel eye—the scornful lip—the expanded nostril, which, like the thorough-bred

Arab's, the slightest excitement brought into activity — seemed to bid defiance to danger; while they also betrayed utter indifference for the sufferings of others.

The conversation which presently began within the hearing of Yanko did not betoken any tenderness for *his* condition, at least. The first words which were spoken by one of a knot who, seated in a circle apart from the rest, appeared to form a special committee on his case, at once arrested the earnest attention of the unhappy captive.

A brass inkstand stuck in his girdle, together with his pistol, showed the speaker to be the Grammatikos, or *homme de lettres* of the company; and this distinction conferred on him the rank of chairman, if such a designation may be used in speaking of a state of society where a chair, or even a stool, is as unknown as were formerly trousers or shirts among the Sandwich islanders.

"Well, Palikaria," said he, "we must

settle now what is to be done with this fellow."

"Oh, *this* will settle him!" interrupted a Klepht who was standing near, busied in sharpening à butcherly knife, which he, in his capacity of messman and cook to the Klephtourià, was accustomed to use in the slaughter of the lambs and kids devoured on high festivals.

"This will do for him beautifully;" and the cruel, hard eye of this *exécuteur des hautes œuvres* twinkled with delight, as he passed the edge of his knife along the inside of his hand. "I'll finish the job at once, and have done with it."

"Not quite so fast, Moré Djezzar Pasha," said the chairman, turning towards the butcher; "no one doubts your skill in cutting a throat, whether of man or beast; but we must know first if no boat has landed at the Krýo-neró. Here comes one who can tell us."

"Well, Kostaki, what news do you bring? Is there nothing in sight?"

A very youthful Klepht—the *boots* of the band, to whom this question was ad-dressed—just then emerging from the tangled wood below the spot where the council was being held, replied, "No-thing. I went down, as you bid me, to the landing-place, and looked all round the bay. There was nothing to be seen on the water, nor was there the splash of an oar to be heard. It is a dead calm. Dhimo the Suliote was at the water-side before the sun went down; he told me he had seen one small sail in the distance, in the direction of Salahora. He is wait-ing there still, in the hope that Photaki Tzavella will arrive in it."

"That's not impossible," observed the Grammatikos, addressing himself to his colleagues. "We had better wait till the dawn; and then, if the boy is not come, let the other's head be taken off."

Among the councillors there stood one whose grey moustache and weather-beaten face gave him the undisputed pre-eminence of age over his younger comrades ; while the condition of his blood-stained, greasy shirt-sleeves, and fustanells, or pet-ticoats, testifying to a confirmed repudiation of soap far beyond the memory of the oldest washerwoman, marked him out as an ancient thief of the purest water. He was viewed by his brother Klephts with a certain degree of awe, from the suspicion generally entertained that he belonged to that variety of the human species furnished by nature with the extraordinary appendage of a *tail*, of which it is asserted that living specimens are to be found at this day in some parts of the Turkish dominions. The peculiarity of his make and stature, and his astonishing pedestrian powers, such as are attributed to men so distinguished, gave rise to the suspicion ; which was, moreover, confirmed by the fact of his being seldom found in a sitting posture.*

"You talk of waiting till to-morrow,"

* *Vide* Note.

said the old Palikari; "but don't you remember that our brave brothers of Suli are all this while waiting for us to come to their assistance? Is it not of greater consequence that we should, without delay, give them the aid of such a band of Palikaria as we, than run the risk of their being eaten up by thousands of those Turkish dogs, for the chance of saving one boy's life?"

While he was speaking, the rest of the band, who had gathered round the fire, were beginning to show signs of impatience; and when he had done, several exclaimed, "That's true; cut his throat, and have done with him."

But when the butcher Klepht, sanctioned by this *plebiscite*, rushed into the cavern to seize his victim, the place was empty—Yanko was no longer there.

"Τὶ ἐγινε το βρωμόσκυλο;—What's become of the dirty hound? Που ἐγλύτωσε ὁ κερατᾶς;—Where is the rascal escaped to?"

At this exclamation, the whole Kleph-

tourià—chairman, committee, and all—
were roused to a state of the most intense
agitation, as a nest of wasps suddenly disturbed in their cells; and some seizing
burning brands from the fire, and others
drawing their swords, all hurried tumultu-
ously to explore the crevices and windings
of the cavern, where alone it was possible
for the prisoner to have secreted himself.
The search was for a long time in vain.
The Klephts became perplexed. Some
were inclined to ascribe the sudden dis-
appearance of their prey to supernatural
agency; and the fancy swelled into superstitious alarm, when a smothered cry was
heard to issue from a remote part of the
cavern, which, to the terror-stricken imagination, sounded like the voice of some
unearthly being, disturbed by the unhal-
lowed intrusion of mortal men.

"'Ο βουρβολὰκ εἶναι," whispered one to
the other; "'T is the ghost!"* The
stoutest hearts quailed at the expectation

* *Vide* Note.

of seeing some horrid phantom arise from the depths of the earth; and all the Klephts stood still in breathless terror— all except the grey-whiskered ancient of the band, who, advancing boldly to the entrance of a lateral passage which had been left unexplored, from which the cry seemed to proceed, and holding up a blazing pine-root which he snatched out of the hand of one of the bystanders, exclaimed with a loud voice,—

"Who is there? Speak again."

There was no answer but the echo of his own voice, and then the sound as of a heavy body falling into water, accompanied by a splashing and floundering noise, and after that a death-like stillness.

The men looked at one another, not daring to speak, as if in doubt of what was to happen next.

Presently the sound as of water falling slowly, drop by drop, into water beneath, struck upon the ears of all.

Again the old Klepht for a moment

felt his flesh creep with a superstitious horror, till, shame and curiosity overcoming his fears, he exclaimed, "May that drop scald thy soul, thou caitiff Vlackh!"* and strode forward, calling on the rest to follow.

His boldness turned the tide against the vourvolak; and now all the band hurried after him along the unexplored passage, which presently terminated in a wide and lofty vaulted chamber, the rocky sides and roof of which, fretted with pendent stalactites, and suddenly lit up by the fitful illumination of so many moving brands, presented the most uncouth and fantastic shapes of "gorgons, and hydras, and chimeras dire."

A part of the floor of this cavern was occupied by a shallow pool, formed by the constant dripping from the roof above. In it there lay, half immersed, something which, in the indistinctness of the visible

* *Vide* Note.

darkness, loomed like the nether hemi-
sphere of a human corpulence.

" There he is at last!" cried the little
butcher, as, lowering his torch to the edge
of the pool, he recognised the carcase of
his longed-for victim. " Thou shalt not
escape the knife, for all thy drowning, my
lambkin," continued he, in the jocular
strain of a laughing hyena, as he twisted
his fingers into the dripping hair of Yanko,
and, lifting the head out of the water,
turned the face up to the light.

The Klephts crowded round the margin
of the basin, to see the better; and as the
red glare of the torches they held aloft fell
flickering upon those ashy features, there
was in them a strange, ghastly, unearthly
expression, which belonged neither to life
nor death—a neutral state, where the immortal spirit seems to be hovering on the
frontiers of both, waiting the snapping
asunder of the last thread by which it still
holds on to its perishable husk. Strange,

indeed, are the reports which some who have been snatched back before crossing the awful confines, have brought of the unseen world beyond.

"Methought," said one recovered from the watery grave, "that a bright cloud rested upon the horizon before me, out of which started, in distinct, vivid reality, every event of my life in the minutest detail, from the earliest recollections of childhood to the recent consciousness of the very last thought which passed through my mind, as I sank into the wave. It seemed as if in that brief moment I lived my whole life over again, and that every minutest incident of the past became, not successively, but *at once,* an actually present reality; just as the entire prospect of earth and ocean, with all its fleeting lights and shadows, the sky and clouds, the sun, and all it shines upon, the countless stars and the illimitable heavens, is, at one glance, distinctly painted on the beholder's eye."

Is it, then, one of the laws of our mysterious nature, that at the instant of the soul's severance from its mortal companion, there is called into action some hitherto latent faculty, by which is fearfully realised to the awakened conscience that dreadful scrutiny announced to all mortal men—" I will set thy sins in array before thee?"

Oh! what a vision of dreadful imagery must have filled the dark chambers of that polluted soul as Angelica's unworthy husband lay entranced in apparent unconsciousness! What a crowd of horrid spectres then hovered round him! and what a shivering shook his coward conscience, as one, the orator of the rest, croaked into his mangled ears, " Welcome to our borders, brother fiend!—we have long waited for thee. Come! assume the place of honour reserved for such as thee—for the dissembling hypocrite, the betrayer of his trust—the ruiner of his benefactor—the oppressor of the orphan

—the rapacious extortioner;—all is ready for thee. Come, come and taste the fruit of thy doings on earth."

The fatal knife was already at Yanko's throat—one gash—one beat the less of the heart's pulse, and the divorce between that prostrate carcass and the departing spirit had been complete, when a sudden outcry was heard at the entrance of the cavern. "He comes!—he comes!" This cry, which the excited imaginations of the Klephts referred to the dreaded vourvolak, revived all their superstitious terrors. At the same instant their brands, damped by the foul air of that pent-up cavern, no longer gave any light. The murky, stifling darkness added to the horror. The knife dropped harmless from the trembling hands of the butcher Klepht into the pool beside his intended victim. Even the grey-whiskered ancient did not escape the contagion of fear.

But presently the sound of Samuel's well-known voice dispelled the illusion.

" Don't kill him—bring him out."   At
this command, issued in a peremptory
tone, enforced by that sternness of will to
which the vulgar instinctively submit as
to a decree of Fate, the body of the half-
drowned Yanko was hastily huddled up
and conveyed to the mouth of the cave,
where the pure, balmy evening breeze,
playing on his ghastly face, gradually
restored him to consciousness.

As he painfully struggled back into life
the dreadful vision still haunted him, and
in the bewilderment and terror of the
reviving sense of his identity he groaned
aloud, " Am I, then, in hell?"   Hell!
hell! hell! was repeated by the echoes,
till the sound died away in the inner
recesses of the cave, and left the hapless
man still more appalled by the silence.

The silence was broken by a rough
voice, "Not yet!" And, when startled and
aroused by this response to his question,
he opened his eyes, expecting to see some
fearful phantom, they fell upon the figure

of one kneeling at his side, who took his hand and respectfully kissed it. He withdrew it, and looked up with a scowl of mingled alarm and repugnance, still doubting the reality of what he saw.

Angelica it was, who, still kneeling, said, in a voice trembling with suppressed emotion,—

"Kyr Nikóla, do you not know me? It is I."

N. "Well, what of that?—who wanted you here?—what are you come here for?"

A. "Sir," she meekly answered, "do you ask? Am I not your wife? Are you not in trouble and in danger? Was it not my duty to come and share both?"

N. "The duty of a wife is to obey her husband—I did not bid you come *here,* woman."

A. "No, Arkhonta! but did you not bid me go to the Vezir, to ——"

N. "Yes; and I warrant you you went gladly enough to parade that face of yours

before *His Highness*," (this he said with
the emphatic sneer of a demon,) "and to
show off your finery and your jewels before the Kokonas of Ioánnina."

" Alas ! " thought Angelica, " he is
wandering !"

" God knows," she replied, " I sought
not the interview, nor could I have dared
to undergo it but at your bidding, and
believing that your life was only to be
saved by the liberation o͑ the Suliote
hostage.   Did not you write to me so?"

N. "Yes, yes; 'tis clear enough. That
Suliote boy was in your eye all the time.
It was not your husband you went to
save;—no, it was that thief's spawn.
You know it was, woman!   But where is
he? for it was under *his* escort, no doubt,
you gave yourself the trouble to come all
this way."

At this base taunt the blood mounted
to Angelica's cheek.   Her lips quivered,
as " with that look which goodness wears
in wrath," she exclaimed, " Ah ! Pa-

nayïamou, sustain me!   Have I deserved this at *his* hands?"

Her clear, open brow was for a moment ruffled into a frown, marking the intensity of the horror with which her pure and candid soul recoiled at such an accusation from the man who called himself her husband.

The Caloyero, who had discreetly kept back during this dialogue, that his presence might impose no constraint upon the expression of conjugal feeling, could no longer contain his indignation.

"Since the days of Nabal, never was there so vile a churl as this," exclaimed he, as he now advanced into the cavern, and stood before Yanko.

"Down on thy knees, dastardly wretch! and worship the guardian angel whose presence saves thee a while from the fate which thy brutality deserves ; for, by all the holy martyrs and saints in heaven, I swear that, but for her whom thou hast so vilely traduced, liar as thou art, thou shouldest not taint the air with the foul venom of thy breath a moment longer."

Samuel's dark eyes kindled like burning coals, and his lips foamed with fury, as he uttered these words. As he stood over the trembling Vlackh with his uplifted arm, his beard and grisly locks red with the glare of the watch-fire, he might have represented the prophet whose name he bore preparing to inflict vengeance on the Amalekite king.

" Spare him!" exclaimed Angelica, and caught the Caloyero's arm; "he is my husband."

" Yea, truly I know it," replied Samuel; " and just because, by his hellish arts, he obtained the right to call thee his wife, the villain deserves to die."

As these words were uttered, Yanko's heart, like the heart of that man of Belial, Abigail's foolish husband, died within him, and became as a stone.

In his terror at this sudden revelation of what he fancied was unknown to all but to his own putrid conscience, Yanko essayed to crawl from where he lay, and catching hold of Angelica's garment, he, on his knees, with a look in which the abject suppliant and detected villain were disgustingly blended, implored in piteous tones the compassion of his insulted, innocent wife.

" Save me! save me!" he whined out; " save me, O wife!—forgive me!—I own I am a wretch. Jewels, money, embroidered clothes—all, all shall be yours, only save my life!"

Wretch, indeed! Did he, then, imagine that the devotedness of such a woman was to be bought by such a bribe?

" Thy money perish with thee!" had been the natural expression of Angelica's just resentment for this fresh aggravation of insult. But it only inspired her with a sense of painful pity for her unworthy husband's degradation, and of shame at its being exhibited before the Klephts, who by this time were hurrying into the

cavern, impatient to know the fate of
Photo from Samuel's lips.

Angelica's first movement was to endeavour to raise Yanko from so unbe-
coming an attitude. " 'Tis not I that can
save you," she said : " do not, sir, kneel
to me, but to God."

As she bent over him, whispering this
exhortation in his ear, the ample cloak in
which she was wrapped dropped from her
shoulders, and displayed her whole figure
arrayed in the costly garments with which
she, so unwillingly, had been attired in the
Vezir's harem, and which, in the hurry of
her flight from its walls, she had not had
time or opportunity to exchange for a less
conspicuous dress.

She was not aware that at that moment
the attention of all the Palikaria was admiringly fixed upon her lovely form. As
she lifted up her eyes from the disgusting
object, uncouthly crouching on the ground
at her feet, she met the eager and intoxi-
cated gaze of those wild, youthful outlaws,

and with a meek and bashful dignity, turning towards Samuel, she said :—

"My father, I am here a defenceless woman; I look to you for protection in the fulfilment of my duty towards my husband."

"Fear not, daughter," replied the old Caloyero to this appeal. "All these you see here are friends, and if need be will be your protectors. They are Hellenes. They have mothers and sisters, whom they are in arms to defend against the common spoiler and oppressor of our country. I know, lady, that you feel as we do, and that you, like us, are thirsting for the liberation of our country from this accursed yoke. The time, perhaps, is not far off when Greek mothers shall be the nurses of free men."

"Palikaria," continued Samuel, turning to the Klephtic band, "this lady is the daughter of one of the greatest benefactors of our nation. You answer for her safety while taking refuge among her fellow-countrymen?"

"That will we!" exclaimed they all, with an enthusiastic shout. "We will defend her from harm at the hazard of our lives."

Oh the awfulness of womanly beauty, when clad in the armour of holy innocence and virtue!

In all that lawless throng there was not one who, at that moment, as he looked on Angelica's pure and modest brow, dared harbour a dishonest thought against her.

Instinctively conscious of the effect produced on them by her presence, and shrinking from their admiring but respectful gaze, she, having acknowledged the expression of their good will by a graceful gesture and a heavenly smile, addressed herself again to the Caloyero: "You must be fatigued, my father, with your kind care of your companion this long, weary day ; and, truth to say, I shall be glad, too, to take some rest."

She approached Kyr Yanko, who during this scene had crawled back to his accustomed nook, purposing to offer her wifely service in dressing his wounds, with such appliances as her compassionate skill could improvisate. But she was repelled by a forbidding motion of his hand, and as the fitful gleam of the bivouac fire was reflected in his small bullet eye, Angelica saw it glare on her with an expression of hate, which made her tongue falter while wishing him a good night. In the meanwhile a couch had been prepared for her in a further corner of the cavern, on a pile of leaves covered with capas, which the Klephts had vied with each other in heaping upon it to protect her from the night air, and then discreetly retired, to leave Angelica to the repose she so much needed.

CHAPTER XLII.

THE night fires had ceased to glimmer, and all was yet gloom and dark within the cavern, when Dhimo came and awoke Samuel, who, wrapped in his shaggy sheep-skin capa, had laid himself down to sleep across the entrance, and might have been mistaken for a gigantic watch-dog. It was with the design of guarding the only approach to his charge, the lovely sleeper within, that he had chosen for his couch that spot, which none could pass without treading upon him. At the first touch of Dhimo, the old Caloyero sprang upon his feet. His first words showed what his last waking thoughts had been.

" Is the boy come?" asked he eagerly.

" No," was Dhimo's disappointing reply.

" Not come yet! Something must

have befallen them by the way; and yet Spiraki is a trusty fellow, and as sharp-witted as a fox. It was a crazy old boat that; and those mountaineers are not used to the water. Well, go back to Lambro and his wife; without him I *can't*. Come what will, I *must* carry their child back to them, dead or alive."

This Samuel said,—half soliloquising, half addressing himself to Dhimo, whose anxiety for the safety of Photo was aroused by that which he saw marked upon the rough features of the old man.

" Why did not Photo come away with you?" said Dhimo.

" Why!" answered the Caloyero, somewhat testily; "why are there such things as women in the world? And yet," added he, after a pause, and in a softened tone, " could I leave the poor innocent ewe lamb at the mercy of that ravening wolf?

" And even now," continued he, inwardly musing, " dare I leave her in the fangs of that swinish wretch, with no protection but that of these lawless scamps, who will be cutting one another's throats for love of her bright eyes, and settle the dispute by killing her?"

Dhimo interrupted Samuel by proposing to go down to the waterside to look, if perchance there were any boat in sight. "The sea-mist," he observed, "prevents any object being discerned from this height."

"Thou say'st well, Dhimo; I will wait here till the Arkhontissa awakes. She might be alarmed to find me gone, after my promise to be her guard till all was settled about her husband's release."

"But what shall we do with *him*," observed Dhimo, "if Photo does not appear? The Klephtourià are becoming impatient. They would have despatched him last evening had you not come."

"Oh! he must not be touched yet, at least," said Samuel, lowering his voice, and looking round to observe if Yanko were awake and listening. "The fellow deserves no mercy; but our only chance of recovering Photo is to have him to give in exchange. But go quick to the seaside and fetch me word."

During this brief dialogue the deep shadows on the mountain-side were beginning to feel the influence of the approaching dawn. Already the mists which had lazily floated along the surface of the Ambracian Gulf, as they gradually rose into mid air, caught a slight tinge of light on the edge turned towards the sunrising, and the craggy outline of Macrinoro, till now undistinguishable amid the dark vapours of the night, was seen quite hard and harsh against the slowly whitening sky.

As Dhimo departed on his errand, Samuel resumed his station to await the waking up of Angelica, who still lay steeped in that deep monumental repose which might suggest the thought of Sleep being the twin-sister of Death.

There was an exquisite grace and calm

expression of holy innocence, which, like the lambent glory of legendary saints hovering upon the features of the lovely sleeper, touched the heart of the old man, with an unwonted tenderness that strangely contrasted with his habitual sternness.

He was presently roused from the reverie into which he was gradually sinking, as he kept watching by that peaceful couch, by a shrill cry, which suddenly came up from the woods beneath, followed, after a short interval, by the crack of a musket-ball, the sharp whizzing sound of which, repeated by the echoes from the impending rocks, was made more startling by the previous deep silence.

The shot was presently followed by another, and then another and another.

Samuel anxiously listened, apprehending that the Klephts had been surprised in their fastness by a sudden invasion of the Pasha's Armatolis. He rushed eagerly out of the cavern, seizing a toufenk that lay on the ground, resolved to make fight; but his alarms were soon dispelled by the exultant cry which struck his delighted ear—"He is come!—Photaki is safe!— Here he is himself!"

This exclamation, repeated by the Klephts, who were soon perceived scrambling from all quarters through the thick trees, was accompanied by an irregular *feu de joie*.

Samuel, as he hastened to meet the joyous band, called out, "Enough, boys! enough! Don't waste your shot—we shall not have more than enough for to-morrow's fight. But where is Tzavella's son?" eagerly he asked of the Palikaria, as they severally emerged from the thicket upon the narrow downward path: "where is the noble boy?"

"He's coming up by the easier path, further on," was the answer returned by the Klepht nearest at hand.

"Has he, then, so soon forgot how to climb the rocks, poor fellow! Oh! how quickly does the foul air of a prison infect the bravest heart!"

"No, no," replied another; "Photo is helping the Bishop to ascend the steep."

"The Bishop!—who?—which?" exclaimed Samuel in surprise.

"He of Arta, to be sure," answered a Klepht. "What other Bishop but he would venture among us? Is he not the friend and protector of all Christian men, Klephts as well as others?"

It was, in very deed, the good, brave Bishop Ignatios, who was presently seen toiling up the path, leaning on Photo, and followed by Dhimo.

Samuel waited till they reached the more level ground from which he first perceived them, and then advanced a few steps to make his obeisance to the prelate, which he did in a style not unlike the bearing of the pirate Duke of Normandy, when doing a vassal's homage to his liege lord, the French King.

The manner of the greeting of the two

ecclesiastics was characteristic of the difference necessarily existing between the
polished prelate and the mountaineer
pastor of a wild flock, the one accustomed
to the forms and semblances at least of
civilized society, with no means to maintain authority over his own people, and to
protect them against the cruelties of their
common oppressor, except by the exercise
of the combined qualities of the serpent and
the dove; the other, wild and rough as a
Druid priest, living the outer life of the
lawless men he had to deal with, and as
prompt to use carnal weapons in leading
them into battle against their foes of flesh
and blood, as to shield them by his spiritual counsels from the assaults of their
ghostly enemies.

Ignatios responded to the rough greeting of the old Caloyero with a gentle
dignity.

"My brother," said he, emphatically
addressing Samuel by this name, to mark
their equality as servants of the same

Master, " you see I have brought our
child thus far safe, and am come to deposit him in your hands. He was confided
to mine on conditions which you must be
told of. But first let me take a little repose to recover my breath after this ascent. We, townsmen," added he, smiling,
" are not used to such rough and steep
paths, — but for my son, Photaki, here, I
should have hardly reached this eagle's
nest."

The young Suliote's eyes glistened with
grateful pride at hearing himself so called
by the Bishop, while Samuel pressed the
boy to his bosom, exclaiming,—

" God be praised ! Now, child, shall
my promise to thy mother be fulfilled."

The Klephts, to whom, in the meantime, Dhimo had communicated the purpose and conditions of his coming, were
crowding round, eager to take a look at
the reverend man, the fame of whose love
for his people and of the generous courage with which he upon all occasions

advocated their interests against the oppression of their task-masters, had en-
deared him to all the Greeks. Every one
seemed desirous to show him respect by
rendering some service, and soon the
zeal of each to be distinguished above
his fellows in the courteous contest rose
to. so fierce a height, that they would
probably have come to blows, each in the
assertion of his prior claim to do honour
to the man of peace, had not the tough
old Caloyero interposed with a peremptory command. "Boys, boys, be men;
leave off your childish quarrelling till after
ye have beaten the Turks. How will ye
ever vanquish the common enemy, as long
as ye are contending who is the greatest
among you?"

"Let the Dhespotes himself speak, and
say what ye can do for him."

"Thanks, thanks, my friends," said
Ignatios; "a draught of milk would be
very grateful to that young lad," he said,
looking towards Photo; "and, indeed, I

should not be sorry to have a sip myself."

The wish was suggested by the sight of a few goats that were browsing among the rocks.

He had hardly spoken the word when there arose a general shout, — " To the Mandra *— to the Mandra!" and in an instant the whole party set off at full speed, like the foot-racers of old in the Stadium, clambering up the steep sides of the mountain, behind the near summit of which they soon disappeared, leaving the Bishop alone with Samuel and Dhimo, to whom he expressed his anxious wish to bring to an immediate conclusion the mission which he had come upon, in order that he might, if possible, get back to Arta in time for the solemn services of the festival.

The glances which passed between the old Caloyero and the Suliote Palikari while the Bishop was speaking, accompa-

* Sheepfold.

nied by those undefinable gestures which form so essential a portion of Greek dialogue — the short-hand of conversation — gave Ignatios to understand that the task he had undertaken was not so easy, or so soon to be accomplished.

"I fear," said Dhimo, in a deferential tone, "that your Holiness may be detained here longer than you wish. 'T is a rare event for such as we to have a Bishop for our guest, and the lads will hardly consent to let you depart without your blessing on this holy day. Although Klephts, we are, Heaven be praised! Christians.

"As for the immediate release of our captive, there is much to be considered before we can consent to that. Your Holiness knows, as well as we, what are the designs of the Pasha against our Suli, and that this Yanko is a needful agent for the furtherance of his schemes. I know, too, O Dhespota, that in your heart you wish us well; and also, that you may be able to defend the poor Rayàhs from

oppression, you must keep on good terms
with our oppressors. We need not disguise from you that the band you now
see assembled in this mountain are preparing for a perilous expedition, to go to
the succour of their brethren of Suli. A
stormy night is what we look for to favour
our march, which lies through the enemy's
country. *Inshallah!*—please God, we
shall have a rare storm before the sun is
down, judging by the looks of the sky
over the sea yonder. By to-morrow's dawn,
I trust, we shall have cut our way through
the Vezir's host to our beleagured friends,
and have restored this brave boy to his
home. Till we make sure of that, we
can't run the risk of letting loose our
hostage to go tell his master how to defeat
our plans."

Ignatios was now fully sensible of the
difficulty of his position, and at once made
up his mind to all its consequences.

The thought he ever nourished in the
depths of his heart was to be instrumental

to the emancipation of his people from the Turkish yoke. He knew this could not be effectually accomplished but by their previous emancipation from the bondage of their own vices and defects;* and he felt that the national leaders in Church and State must themselves set the example of that pure, highminded self-sacrifice—that ὑψηλοψυχία, which constitutes the living spirit of true patriotism. He therefore refrained from any allusion to the danger he had personally and voluntarily incurred by the pledge given to Alỳ Pasha, to bring back either Yanko or Photo; and replied to the Suliote Palikari's speech by saying,—

"You say well, Dhimo; and since, by God's providence, I have been brought among these few stray sheep wandering in the desert, who have been unused to the voice of a faithful pastor, we will together offer up our prayers and praises to our Heavenly Father. It will not be

* *Vide* Note.

the first time that caves and rocks have served instead of a church to poor Christians."

Samuel had remained all this while seated on the ground, watching Photo, who lay asleep at the edge of the leafy couch prepared for the Bishop. The latter, addressing himself to the Papàs, said, "If you, brother, will undertake the office of deacon, and prepare what can be prepared in this wild place for the Divine worship, God will accept our humblest service, when given with a willing heart. I will gladly snatch a few minutes' sleep, like that poor child."

The Papàs immediately arose, and, with a reverential gesture of assent, made straight for the cavern, to execute, as well as he could, the episcopal commission.

What, meanwhile, had become of the ill-yoked couple, who were left to take their repose apart in that gloomy chamber? Repose! What repose can he enjoy, who lays himself down in his bed with

the expectation of being called up at daylight by the executioner?

Fain would Yanko have shut out from
his thoughts the anticipated miseries of
the coming morrow, by closing his eyes to
the light that still flickered, with just
power enough to deepen the gloom of the
cavern, which above and around him
seemed to stretch out into an immeasur-
able abyss of visible darkness. If at last,
exhausted with the wanderings of his own
terrified fancy, he sank into a momentary
slumber, it was only to be overridden by
a heavy nightmare, that danced a hurricane galop over his labouring breast,
keeping time to a chaotic dream, in which
the wretched man beheld himself set up
as a target to be shot at with flaming bul-
lets, cast in the foundry of hell, by a pla-
toon of demon Palikaria, who, under the
command of Photo, awaited the signal to
fire from his wife Angelica.

By that strange, inexplicable sympathy,
or coincidence between the facts of the

waking world and the dreamer's phan-
tasmagoria, the rattle of the Klephtic
feu de joie, which announced the arrival
of Photo, chiming in with the visionary
volley, roused Yanko from his dream.

When, after one last desperate, convulsive struggle with the superincumbent
goblin, he started from his couch, the im-
pressions of his dream still pursued him
across the shadowy frontier which divides
sleep from perfect wakefulness, until they
at length, like ghosts at cock-crow, vanished before the light of day.

The first object that arrested his view
was the figure of Angelica, who still lay
plunged in the sweet oblivion of a profound and gentle sleep—calm, silent, and
pale, as if she were already laid in the
tomb.

As Yanko approached his wife, half
doubting whether her spirit were yet a
tenant of that lovely frame, he could perceive a smile dimpling her cheek, and her
lips slightly apart, as if essaying to speak.

"Σωτηρεμου, ἐρχομαι—I come, my Sotiri!*—I come!" were the words she
whispered, as Yanko bent forward to catch
the faint sound, impelled by that malig-
nant curiosity which seeks to draw from
every breath, and look, and gesture of the
injured victim, wherewith to envenom and
justify the hatred of the oppressor.

If there was one name more than another which grated harshly on the ears of
the Vlackh's conscience, it was that of
Sotiri—the deeply-loved, the ever-remem-
bered, the basely-betrayed brother of his
injured wife. The startling resemblance
which Photo bore to Sotiri, in person, in
features, in voice, in gait, had struck
Yanko with an undefinable misgiving,
from the first moment that the Suliote
hostage was consigned to his unwilling
custody by Alỳ Pasha. That resemblance,
which naturally awakened in Angelica's
loving heart so deep an interest for the
young Klepht, and which, in her guile-

* *Vide* Note.

lessness, she had never thought of concealing, only made her husband hate them both more cordially, and, with the instinctive logic of that rotten thing, the intellect of a foul heart, ground his right to hate on the consciousness of his deserving both hatred and scorn.

In this temper it was that Yanko heard the name of Sotiri breathed by the lips of his wife in her sleep.

"Curse on that name!" muttered he to himself; "I wish there were no such name in the calendar. Sure I am she is dreaming of that Klephtopoulo, and calls him by her brother's name. She is like all women—a dissembler even in her sleep. And yet, how quietly she sleeps!"

As he kept gazing, and trying to goad himself with his own wolfish fancies into the belief of his having a real grievance against that innocent lamb, he felt only the more irritated at the tranquillity of the repose, which so contrasted with the perturbation of his own mind.

"But what is that jewel in her hair?" exclaimed he; "that is the very diamond I presented to the Vezir when ——"

The conclusion of the sentence stuck in his throat; but it was articulated by the tongue of his conscience loud enough to make his soul tremble.

"When thou didst purchase the Vezir's sufferance of thy villany with that same jewel—part of the orphan's fortune entrusted to thy guardianship by her confiding father ——"

He looked suspiciously towards the opening of the cavern, to see whether any one were near. All was still.

"Well," continued he, in converse with himself, "since there it is, I'll take back my own."

He had just succeeded in detaching it from her fair brow, when he heard the steps of some one approaching. He hastily thrust the prize into his bosom, and slunk back to his couch, where he had no sooner laid himself down in a counterfeit sleep, than with his half-closed eyes, and trembling lest he should be noticed, he saw Samuel stalk in, and go straight towards the spot where Angelica still lay in placid repose.

" 'T is a pity to awake her, poor sufferer !" murmured the priest to himself, as he came and looked upon her; "yet it is not right she should remain here exposed, in broad day, to the gaze of these wild Palikaria."

While he hesitated for a moment to disturb her, Angelica awoke; and as the returning consciousness of the sad realities of life broke in upon her, she heaved a long, deep sigh, and looking up, saw the old man's face bending over her with an expression of loving commiseration.

"Is it you, Babàm?" she said; "I fear your watchfulness for me has deprived you of your needful rest."

"No matter, Kyrà. Sorry am I to disturb your slumbers; but the spot you have been resting upon is to serve us for

an altar for the worship of to-day's festival, which Bishop Ignatios is presently
to celebrate, 'with the Palikaria for his
congregation."

Yanko, who, unnoticed, was listening
from his corner with intense curiosity to
catch every word, would have pricked up
his ears, had they been there, at hearing
the name of the Bishop of Arta. " What
can he be come here for?" thought he.
" Has he, too, fallen into the hands of
these thieves? or has he been sent for
my ransom ?"

To Angelica, the mention of the good
Bishop's name, and of his being actually
near at hand, brought a gleam of joyful
hope, which she could not conceal.

"Oh! that I could be allowed to see
him, and tell him all that is in my heart!"
she exclaimed.

" Well, I thought of that, too," said
the Caloyero. "I know he will be glad
to know you, Kyrà; and you may speak

boldly and confidently to him. There is
no fear of his not giving *you* absolution :
for though I know little of you women,
I doubt me whether there be many like
Agathopoulo's daughter. Come with me ;
I will lead you to his Holiness ; and what
is more, you shall see one who, but for
your courage, brave daughter, would by
this time have perished, as well as *he* of
whom I will not now speak. 'T is Photo
Tzavella, I mean. Well, lady, what!
are you not pleased that the lad is alive
and safe here within a few paces of this
very spot?"

Angelica at first could not speak. She
had fallen upon her knees, and covered
her face with her hands, giving no utterance to the emotions which swelled her
heart but by tears and sobs; and then,
at last, by broken words of thanksgiving
to the Deliverer of the captive, and the
Comforter of the broken-hearted,—

"Pardon me, my father," said she, as

she rose from her knees; "I am not ungrateful; my heart was too full. Such joy as God has granted me is a serious thing. Pray lead me to his Holiness."

CHAPTER XLIII.

ANGELICA had a misgiving, as she followed Samuel out of the cavern, that her husband, though apparently asleep, had been all the time watching her movements. As she looked back, half dreading to see him at her heels and to feel his grasp, her rapid glance caught sight of his head bent forward, and of the dull twinkle of his eye fixed upon her.

She shuddered like one who suddenly lights upon a snake, and hurried on to the spot where Bishop Ignatios was taking his scanty measure of repose, with the young Suliote fast asleep by his side.

" There's no time to stand upon ceremonies," said Samuel to Angelica, who was shrinking back, as fearing to disturb their slumbers. " The lads will soon be

down from the mandra. There's not a
minute to spare, if you wish to speak with
the Dhespotés before they can come and
interrupt you."

So saying, the sturdy old Priest pulled
his Holiness familiarly by the sleeve ; but
as he looked down upon Photo, he said,——

" Poor fellow ! let *him* have his sleep
out. See how he smiles !—he is very
likely dreaming of *you*, lady."

" More likely of his mother," observed
Angelica. " Alas ! many a sleepless night
must she have passed, poor soul ! thinking
of that boy."

When Ignatios was forced back from
the land of dreams by the vigorous operations of the impatient Papàs, his eyes,
slowly and wearily opening, first met the
lovely figure of Angelica standing before
him.

Such an apparition, in the midst of
that wild scenery, so unexpected and so
out of place, would, doubtless, have been
deemed by anchorites of old as among

the Satanic delusions, which, under the semblance of a heavenly vision, were wont to be practised by the tempter on those saintly savages.

If the good Bishop had any doubt of the substantial reality of the apparition, it was quickly dispelled by Samuel, who, taking Angelica by the hand, presented her to him.

" O Dhespota!" said he, " here is a poor lamb snatched from the jaws of the wolf, who comes to you for counsel and comfort. Kyrà Angelica is the daughter of a man whose name is dear to every Hellenic Christian heart. Who has not heard of Agathopoulo of Salonica? It is in the fulfilment of a perilous duty that she, Kyr Yanko's wife, has ventured hither under my escort. She wishes to consult your Holiness' in private."

Samuel, having thus performed his part of master of ceremonies, discreetly withdrew, to leave Angelica at liberty to pour out her heart without constraint into the

ears of her ghostly counsellor. While
the Papàs was speaking she had kneeled
down, and putting the hem of the episcopal robe to her lips, awaited the result
with downcast eyes.

Ignatios remained silent a few minutes,
thoughtfully scanning the features of that
beautiful face before him, as if he were
tracing in them the resemblance of some
loved one.

" Yes, I see thou must be, in very
deed, the daughter of my earliest and
dearest friend!" he exclaimed, in deep
emotion. " How strange that I should,
for the first time, meet his child in such
a spot as this! and she, the wedded wife
of him I am come hither to redeem from
captivity! Fear not, Kyrà Angelica,
trust in me, as if I were indeed your
father; tell me all that is in your heart."

The confiding expression with which
she looked up in the good man's face,
and the fervour with which she kissed

his hand, spoke all her gratitude. Her
lips trembled as she faintly said,—

"O sir! oh, that you could guess all
that is in my poor lonely heart! all that
I would, yet dare not, utter! I am too
unhappy!"

The memories of her father and brother, and once happy home, passed over
her spirit like a dark cloud, and she
burst into an agony of tears.

The Bishop remembered the saying of
the wise king, that the heart's bitterness
is known only to itself. "Would that I
could sweeten the cup for thee, poor sufferer!" was the wish which rose to his
lips; but he patiently waited in expressive silence the subsidence of the heart-
storm, which he felt was not to be con-
trolled by the mawkish truisms of common-place consolation. The tearful eye,
the loving look, the friendly pressure of
the hand, the suppressed sigh, are the
only language which goes home to the

bosom of the weeping sufferer, strengthening while it softens and calms.

And so it was with poor Angelica — soothed and fortified by the unuttered sympathy of her father's friend, she gradually recovered her composure, and then briefly and simply related all that had happened from the evening when she received, by the hands of Samuel, the written command of her husband to present herself before the Vezir at Ioánnina to the moment when she made her escape from the harem, through the contrivance of the faithful Arghyrousa.

" I tremble at the thought of what has befallen that devoted creature," continued Angelica. " I was too hurried and bewildered to think of aught but the risk of being immured within those horrid walls; and the moment I found myself free, my first and ruling thought was to join my husband wherever he might be. I remembered my father's words, that there is safety nowhere but in the path of duty."

" Thou hast nobly done thy duty, my daughter," said the Bishop, who had listened to her narrative with the deepest interest. " Thou art the worthy child of thy excellent father. God will reward thee. Thou wilt experience the faithfulness of the declaration, that *all* the paths of the Lord are mercy and truth unto such as keep his covenant and his testimonies. Surely it is in mercy that our steps have been directed hither by His providence, to redeem the lives of the two captive hostages, this boy and your husband.

" Their exchange will—*Inshallah!*—be soon settled ; and then, lady, you will return, happy in the consciousness of the good you have effected, in peace to your home."

A slight shudder passed over Angelica, as, with a faint smile, she repeated the

Bishop's words, " Peace at home!" and lifted up to heaven a look, which seemed to say, There is no peace for me but in that home above!

It was thus that Ignatios, who watched every movement of hers with the anxious tenderness of a parent by the bed-side of a sick child, interpreted that look.

" Fear not, dear lady," said he, taking her hand, and replying to her heart's unuttered misgivings; " fear not, a happier time awaits you. If Kyr Nikóla has been so unhappy till now as not to appreciate the worth of such a wife, the proof which your presence here furnishes of your devotion to your duties, such as few wives would give, must make him feel what a treasure he possesses."

A mournful shake of her head expressed Angelica's dissent from this inference.

" Alas! my Lord Bishop," she said, " would I could flatter myself as you too kindly do. But when your Holiness learns

that my coming here has been turned by
Kyr Yanko into a ground of accusation
against me,—and *what* an accusation ....!"

Angelica's lips quivered with emotion.
A burning blush swept across her smooth
pale brow, like a blood-red sun-gleam
colouring the marble statue of a Grace,
while the keen resentment of the foul
insult, which lay hidden in her woman's
heart, was revealed in a flash of indignant
scorn, that shot from the dark-blue depth
of her speaking eyes like a sudden thunder-clap from the serene heavens.

"I will not deceive you, my Lord
Bishop," resumed Angelica, in a firm
and solemn tone, which singularly contrasted with the feminine tenderness and
timidity of her usual manner. "I have
tried to love my husband; but he will
not let me: he has ever repelled the
attempts I have made, since, in obedience
to my blessed father's dying wish I became his wife, to win his affections. I
will persevere in my duty to the last, so

God help me; but I will not degrade myself by any reply to the base suspicions of one who knows in his heart how false and groundless they are. Will it be believed that that poor child by your side is also the innocent object of his rooted aversion? Your Holiness, no doubt, knows of the Suliote hostage having been sent to our house in the mountains by command of the Vezir, for the recovery of his health. Who could see a poor child so wan, so wretched, so desolate, without feeling compassion for him?

" I had a brother once, Dhespota, of the same age, and so like this poor Photo in person, voice, and manner, that I almost was deluded into the belief that he was the same. Oh, that he were, indeed, my own dear brother, that I might yield him all a true sister's love!"

Angelica was not conscious, while she was speaking, that, besides the Bishop, there was another listener, who drank up each syllable she uttered with the greediness of a wanderer who comes upon a spring in the desert. It was Photo: he awoke from his sleep as Angelica began her narrative to the Bishop. He was hardly conscious whether he were in a dream; but when assured of the reality of her presence, he lay at first entranced and soothed by the sweet tones of her voice, and then, becoming more and more interested in the subject of which he formed a part, his excitement at hearing himself mentioned by those lips with so compassionate a tone admitted of no restraint, and suddenly starting from his rough couch, he sprang upon his feet, and, with a passionate gesture, was going to seize her hand, when his ardent gaze encountered in her pure and alarmed look and in her retiring attitude, so gentle and yet so effectual a rebuke of his ardour, that he suddenly restrained himself, and turning to the Bishop, he said,—

"O Dhespota! Kyrà Angelica has not told you all. She has been more than a sister to me; she is my guardian angel: but for her I might have disgraced the name of Suliote. 'Twas she that strengthened me when I for a moment wavered, fearing for *her* life, and bid me suffer all rather than fail in my integrity. Oh, that I were, indeed, her own brother! May not I love her as if I were so?"

The Bishop was spared the necessity of resolving so delicate a point of the heart's casuistry by the sudden irruption of Samuel, who advanced with hurried step and perturbed countenance, exclaiming,— " He is not to be found! Where can he have hid himself? I have sought him in every corner of the cave. The Palikaria will soon be here. If they find him out of bounds, woe betide him!"

" Who?" said the Bishop. " Who?"

" Who?" cried the old Priest, impatiently. " Who but that . . . . ?"

All this time Samuel's eyes kept moving from side to side with the keen exploring glance of an Indian backwoodsman, when, all of a sudden, he made a dart over the end of the couch on which the Bishop had been reposing, and disappearing behind the tangled bushes that fringed the steep declivity beneath, he was presently heard to roar out, at the gruffest top of his voice,—

" I see him! I have got him! Come along, Kyr Nikóla! come! Everybody is waiting for you."

Angelica's misgiving had not deceived her. Yanko, curious to know what his wife had to say to the Bishop, had stolen by a lower path to the spot from which he was now unearthed, and there had heard every word which she, unconscious of such a listener, had spoken.

He, making a desperate effort to elude the powerful grasp of the redoubtable Papàs, lost his footing on the rocky ledge where he had been ensconced, and was only saved from rolling down the rough precipice by seizing the stem of the nearest shrub, with the help of which and of an auxiliary shove *à tergo*, lent him with no gentle hand by Samuel, he wriggled himself into a secure but most undignified position.

A more ghastly or more repulsive object was never presented to the sight of man or woman, than that which now, in the unwashed, unshaven, and mangled form of Kyr Nikóla, was at length seen emerging, with a convulsive scramble, from among the tangled, thorny underwood, upon the narrow platform where were grouped together Angelica, Ignatios, and Photo, leaving but a scanty space for a fourth *dramatis persona*.

The bandages had been stripped off in his conflict with the briers, and were floating in shreds on the branches; his clothes were torn to tatters; and the squalid appearance of his whole person bore testimony to the discomforts he had endured since his abduction from his own warm home. It was no little aggravation of his misery that he found himself thus

suddenly thrust into the presence of the
Bishop, in a plight that the meanest
beggar would have been ashamed of.

The unexpected apparition of one, the
Vezir's confidant, whom the Bishop had
been accustomed to meet in the halls of
the seraï, treated by the Vezir's courtiers
with the deference usually paid, under
most *régimes*, to prosperous knaves, produced on Ignatios anything but an agreeable impression.

What between disgust at the mean-
ness of the eavesdropper, pity at the wretchedness of Yanko's appearance, and a pru-
dent recollection of the value set upon
his release by the despot whose commission he was come to fulfil at the risk of
his own safety, Ignatios was embarrassed
in what manner to accost the unwelcome
intruder. As for Angelica, she involun-
tarily shrank back at the ghastly expression of that too-well-known face; but the
instinct of her compassionate and gentle
nature coming in aid of her abiding sense

of wifely duty, she was casting in her mind how best to minister to his relief, when the appearance of another actor upon the stage—Papàs Samuel—gave another direction to the conduct of the drama. Yanko no sooner caught a glimpse of his relentless pursuer, than he, still in the grovelling attitude from which he had not yet had time to raise himself, seized the skirts of the Bishop's robe, appealing to him in a most lamentable strain, the burden of which was,—

" *Amàn, Amàn!* Κυριε ελεησον" (Kyrie-eleyson).

" Thou may'st well cry '*Amàn*,' " said Samuel, looking down upon the abject supplicant with ineffable contempt. " Why dost thou not cling to thy *wife's* skirts? for *her* presence along protects thee from the fate thou hast all thy life worked hard to deserve. Thou hast been treache-rously listening to *her* confession. Hast thou heard a syllable that an angel could be ashamed to utter? Now, she shall hear *thy* confession, thou worse than devil!"

"*Amàn, Amàn!*" howled Yanko, turning to the inexorable Caloyero, and catching hold of his feet, which he would have kissed, had not Samuel stepped back in evident disgust.

"Don't kneel to me, man!" exclaimed he. "Lay hold of the mercy-seat of Him who alone can pardon thy wickedness, as He alone knows its full extent."

"*Amàn, Amàn!*" again repeated Yanko, turning for protection to Angelica.

But she, overpowered with shame at her husband's degradation, and yet commiserating his wretchedness, had retired a few paces, and sat herself down on a stone, hiding her face in her hands. Once she cast an imploring look to Samuel, her eyes streaming with tears. His words were in reply to that look, which sought him to spare her unworthy husband.

"No, lady, no. Thou dost not know

the villany by which thou wert betrayed into the hands of this miserable reptile."

"*Amàn, Amàn!*" again shrieked Yanko. "I confess it all! I avow everything you command!"

Angelica, her heart bursting with sobs, exclaimed, "I do not wish to know anything. He is my husband. Oh, spare him! spare me this agony!"

Samuel waved impatiently his hand towards Angelica, who, despairing of arresting the torrent of his aroused indignation, turned away her head in deep despondency, and stopped her ears with her hands, to escape, if possible, the terror of the avowal which the remorseless Samuel seemed resolved to wring from Yanko.

"Answer me," said he, as he turned to the wretched man, who lay crouching on the ground like a dog that fears a beating, "answer me, as thou wilt have to answer at the day of judgment,—Didst thou not, reptile as thou art, worm thyself into the confidence of her father" (and he pointed to Angelica), "for the sole purpose of betraying him to his ruin, and then of getting possession of his wealth? Answer me, Yes or No?"

"*Amàn, Amàn!*" was the only reply.

"Didst thou not, in the delirium of his last illness, get him to sign a paper by which he made you guardian of his orphan children, and laid a dying injunction on his daughter to become thy wife? And was it not by the exhibition of that paper, which you drew up, and which he never read, that that angel, thinking she obeyed the will of her loved father, consented to become allied to such a beast as thou?"

"*Amàn, Amàn!*"

"No, no; '*Amàn*' won't do. Confess distinctly and precisely, in presence of my Lord Bishop of Arta, that what I say is literally and exactly true."

"It is all quite true," groaned out Yanko, with a sob that might have softened the heart of a crocodile.

"One more question, and I have done," continued Samuel. "Tell me, thou *guardian* of thy benefactor's orphan children, didst thou not knowingly and purposely expose her brother, her only relation, her only friend on earth, to the infection of the plague, by which he perished? Speak, villain! are not these things true? — Thou thoughtest verily that they were hid from the knowledge of men; but didst thou not know that the eyes of God were upon thee, and that for all these things thou shalt be called to judgment? Speak, wretch! darest thou deny the truth of any one of these facts?"

"*Amàn, Amàn!*" again groaned out the miserable caitiff. "It is all true, all very true. *Amàn, Amàn!*"

"Fall now on thy knees," exclaimed Samuel; "make thy confession to the Bishop, who has been witness to all thou hast avowed, and seek for absolution at his hands. But hark ye, while I add yet one word more. Thou hast now learnt, to thy surprise doubtless, that thou art known to be what thou really art—a villain. Know this, further, that if thou . shouldst hereafter, and in revenge of the truth now brought to light, lift up thy hand against that angel wife of thine, or utter one harsh word against her . . . ."

Here the terrible Priest lifted up his arm with a menacing gesture, and seemed on the point of prematurely acting the threat which, in his wrath, he could not find words severe enough to utter. It was arrested by a sudden shout from the impending crag of the mountain, and at the same instant was heard a hollow, rumbling sound of huge fragments of rock, which came crashing, and leaping, and bounding madly down its side, tearing up the soil, and crushing everything in its way.

Photo, during the scene which has

been just described, had watched the actors in it with the most intense interest. He was the first to perceive the danger that threatened the life or the limbs of all those who remained on that narrow stage. At one bound he was at Angelica's side, and seizing her by the arm, dragged her hurriedly from the spot, and lifted her into a secure position upon a block of stone, protected by a jutting ledge of rock from the avalanche of stones which kept pouring down from the higher ground, as they were set in motion by the descending Klephts.

The glances exchanged at this critical moment between Angelica and the young Suliote, expressive of gratitude on her part and of exultation on his at her escape from the peril, did not pass unobserved by Yanko, whose watchful jealousy was not laid asleep by the care of his own person, which he now hastened to lodge in a place of safety by precipitately retiring to his prison nook in the cavern.

The louder and louder shouts of the Klephts announced their nearer and nearer approach, and soon they appeared crowding on the narrow pathway that led past the niche in which Angelica had taken refuge. Before she had time to step down from it, and follow the Bishop and Samuel, who, like Yanko, had retreated into the cavern, the Palikaria, turning a projecting rock which hid her from their view, came suddenly upon her.

There was not one who, as that lovely vision burst upon him, but would have lingered to gaze on in thrilling admiration, had he not been pushed forward by the throng that followed.

There was in the attitude and look of Angelica that graceful awkwardness which betrayed the consciousness she could not but have of the admiration she excited, and would have shrunk from. That consciousness was succeeded by a feeling of alarm when the last youth of the band stopped, fell on his knees, and gazed with a boldly passionate look upon her face.

The *adoration* of personal beauty has ever been in the Greek mind an intense passion, a παϑος, an inordinate affection, amounting to idolatry. There is no excess to which that, in them an almost irrepressible instinct, allied as it is to a host of kindred inflammable passions, jealousy, desire, revenge, will not hurry the Greek.*

To find herself the object, as it were, of such worship, was alike revolting to Angelica's sentiments of feminine modesty and of piety.

In her anxiety to escape from further notice, she hastily stepped from her pedestal, and hurried past the still kneeling Palikari, who, even after she disappeared from his sight, still fixed his gaze on her footsteps, just as one entranced by some exquisite melody continues to listen, after it has ceased to vibrate on his ear. Presently the young Klepht, suddenly start-

* *Vide* Note.

ing on his feet, and pushing rudely aside
Photo, who stood in his path, sprang forward after Angelica.

Photo marked his ardent look and
frantic gesture, and thought he perceived
an expression of fierce scorn in his lip and
in his glance as he passed him.

The Klepht was Photo's elder by three
or four years—a splendid specimen of
that beauty which approaches the strength
of full manhood, still retaining some of
the graceful freshness of youth. But there
was in his eye, and mouth, and in his
whole person, the expression of a reckless,
sensual, profligate mind, from which the
pure and the innocent instinctively shrink,
—the *adorable mauvais sujet* of a corrupt
society — and which awoke in Photo's
heart, nettled by the Palikari's rudeness
and scornful glance, a strange misgiving
that the man was frenzied with a dishonest passion for Angelica. Photo felt
as a brother would feel at seeing a loved
sister insulted by the pursuit of such an

admirer. The suspicion gave wings to the speed with which he instantly ran after the Klepht, who, hid for a moment as well as Angelica from his view by a turn of the path, was at the next seen snatching at the hand of the fugitive, while she, as she grasped the twisted roots of a tree that stuck out of the rifts of the rock, repelled her pursuer's touch with evident disgust.

The sight stung Photo to madness: his dark eye flashed fire. Who had met its glance at that moment might fancy he had seen embodied in it a human soul, winged with all the passions that make man more terrific than a wild beast, rushing on to deadly revenge. With the bound of a chamois he cleared in an instant the space that separated him and its object.

" Touch but the skirt of her garment with a finger, and I will . . . ."

He completed the sentence with a thrust of his elbow, as he pushed between the Klepht and Angelica, whom at the same moment, fainting with emotion and exhaustion, he saved from sinking to the ground by catching her in his arms.

The Klepht lost his footing from the blow, and as he endeavoured to recover himself, and to disentangle his pistol from the folds of his girdle, he muttered,—

"I may not touch her garment with one of my fingers, sayest thou, puny boy? But this ball shall touch her heart, and thine too."

Before he had time to effect his murderous purpose, it was frustrated by Samuel, who from the cavern's mouth had observed the flight and the pursuit, and suspecting mischief would ensue between the two hot-blooded youths, hastened to prevent it. He was just in time to strike the pistol from the Klepht's hand with the heavy staff, which was the old Priest's constant companion.

The pistol fell rattling down the steep below.

"Begone, boy!" said he in a peremptory

tone, that brooked no resistance; "go seek thy weapon, and learn to use it more worthily. Had I flung thee down after it, 'twere no more than thou deservest for lifting it against a comrade. Go and join the rest, and like them prepare thy soul and thy arms against to-morrow's fight. Thou may'st then exhibit thy pluck against the enemy, instead of disgracing thyself by shooting at women. Go!"

The young man slunk away, ashamed, at the stern and contemptuous rebuke of the old Priest. He who had read the thoughts of revenge that were working in his soul, as he turned his back upon the scene of his humiliation, would have done Photo good service by bidding him beware.

But Photo was too much occupied with his precious burthen to heed aught else now. With the support of Samuel's stalwart arm, Angelica was conveyed into the cavern, and laid carefully upon the couch on which she had passed the night.

The Bishop meanwhile having taken a seat near to where Yanko lay, was watching an opportunity to say a few words which might bring that miserable man to a sense of that truth of which it has been said, "HELL *is Truth perceived too late.*"

CHAPTER XLIV.

ANGELICA slowly recovered from the faintness which succeeded to the agitation caused by the revelation of her wretched husband's iniquities, and by her narrow escape from the violence of the profligate Palikari. As her eyes turned towards the light, which was now streaming brightly down the dark throat of the cavern, the first object which they fell upon was the figure of Ignatios, who stood at a short distance from the couch on which she lay. His clasped hands, the slight motion of his lips, and his eyes turned heavenwards, gave indication of his being engaged in mental prayer; and Angelica *felt*, as she fixed her gaze upon the sweetly sad expression of his face, that *she* was the subject of his silent petition. In this she was confirmed by the look which met hers, as Ignatios, perceiving her to be now fully sensible of his presence, spoke words of encouragement and hope, addressed to her inmost, but unuttered, thoughts.

" Fear not, my child; God knows thy path, and will guide thee through. Put thy trust in Him. I have prayed for thee, and for *him*, too" (and he glanced towards the opposite side, where Yanko was crouching, as if to hide himself).

Angelica could only make answer by a long-drawn sigh. All the surmises and misgivings, which she had so long struggled against and endeavoured to cast out, with respect to her husband's delinquencies, had been more than confirmed by his avowal of them all that morning. The illusions with which she had tried to disguise from herself the dreadful reality, had been torn to tatters by the rough hand of the plain-spoken Samuel; and Yanko stood convicted by his own confession of being the betrayer of her father, the murderer of her brother, and the swindler of her fortune and person. A doubt for the first time shot across her desponding heart, whether to live under the same roof with that violator of all laws, human and divine, were a sacrifice strictly demanded· of her by the most· scrupulous sense of wifely duty.

" I will consult this holy Bishop," was the whisper of her perplexed heart, " and abide by his decision. Perhaps he may point out to me a safe refuge in some convent of pious women, where I may spend my remaining days (oh that they may be few!) in preparing for the rest which is only to be found beyond these clouds of earth."

This resolution was a balm to her wounded spirit, and she looked up to her father's friend with that confidence of a guileless heart which gave to her expressive eyes a pure lustre, such as one may suppose to have shone in the eyes of the pri-

vileged little children, when they artlessly
gazed on the divine lineaments of Him
who took them in His arms and blessed
them.

But the current of her thoughts was
presently diverted into another channel
by the appearance of the whole Klephtic
band, whom Samuel had, in the meanwhile, been calling together to the church
service.

Their approach was heralded by wild,
shrill cries, and snatches of Klephtic *tra-
goudhia*, which echoed through the woods
and against the rocks, more like the yells
of prowling jackals than the voices of
human beings. Who that has once heard
the startling discords which composed the
harmony of those untamed colts of freedom, can have forgotten them, or can desire to hear them again? Discordant as
they were, they were not without their
charm for those who knew that the songs
and the melody were but the natural
expression of hearts fiercely panting for

release from the thraldom of a brutal despotism. Thus did they sound in the ears of Angelica, nurtured as she had been, from her earliest infancy, in the hope of witnessing the emancipation of her race, and perhaps of contributing to it by the example of the virtues which adorn the free woman.

The Bishop, when aware of the approach of the men, went and took his station near the rude altar which Samuel had arranged, as well as the scanty means at his disposal allowed. It was a piece of rock, which, jutting out some way into the middle from the side of the cavern, afforded a sufficiently flat surface, on which the Caloyero had spread his own sheepskin capa, and over that the long coarse cotton towel, which, when twisted like a cable, formed his own head-gear.

In the middle he had contrived to erect a cross, rudely formed of two branches tied together by a rope; and in fissures at each end of the rock he had stuck

two fragments of pine-root, to do service
for more orthodox tapers.

The pencil of Salvator Rosa were better
fitted than the pen of the writer to de-
scribe the strange and solemn wildness
of the spot in which the Bishop Ignatios
and the band of Klephts were now met
together.

Instead of the fair-proportioned cathedral, with its clustered pillars, its high-
pointed arches, its fretted roof, and all
the quaint devices of human art, symbo-
lising divine mysteries, and laid out according to man's puny measure, imagine
a vast, uncouth, Cyclopian cave, roughly
scooped out of the granite ribs of Pelion
or Ossa by the giant arms of the sons of
earth, seeking for weapons in their strike
against cloud-compelling Jove. Then suppose the insurgent operatives, suddenly
overtaken by the bolts of the Thunderer,
obliged to abandon their unfinished bar-
ricade, leaving huge fragments of rock
half-torn away from the sides of the

mountain, and the rest strown in wild confusion over the floor of the cavern.

To the mind conversant with the classic myths of ancient Greece, such fancies might have been suggested by the scene where the Christian pastor now stood, face to face with his impromptu flock.

It was, truly, not a flock of *lambs;* yet as Ignatios slowly and silently surveyed those fierce martial countenances, there was something in his meek and thoughtful, but undaunted eye, which, as it met theirs, seemed to quell for a moment the fierceness of their natures. For as, reaching the entrance of the cavern, each one by one caught sight of the altar, and the cross, and the lighted tapers, and the venerable man standing by, the shouts and cries with which they had provoked the echoes instantly ceased; and every Klepht devoutly crossing himself, knelt down, and looking up into that calm, courageous face, waited in a reverential attitude the beginning of the solemnity, with an awkward consciousness of the unwonted novelty of the scene and action in which he was called on to bear a part.

Nor was Ignatios's position without its novelty and embarrassment.

There was he, a Rayàh—that is, a subject of the Sultan — holding communion with men in avowed rebellion against the Sultan's authority. A Greek himself, bowed under the same odious yoke which his lawless compatriots were openly essaying to break and cast off, all his sympathies, his wishes, and his hopes, were on their side, whilst his relation to the Sovereign under whose sanction he held the episcopal authority, which he exercised in his diocese, imposed on him the duty of rebuking and repressing the designs which he knew these men were at that moment nourishing for the recovery of their national freedom. Ignatios was also conscious that he had in Kyr Nikóla Yanko an unfriendly auditor, and a keen spy on the watch for every look, and gesture, and word, which he might, in due time, and with no lack of *charitable* comment, report to their common master, the vindictive Alỳ.

But he of Arta was not the man to be swayed by any considerations about his own safety when engaged in what he deemed to be his duty, and at that moment a deep sense of his responsibility as a Christian pastor made him insensible to every danger but that which imperilled the salvation of the immortal beings, whose eyes he was conscious were fixed upon him with an earnest gaze, as of men looking for a sign from heaven.

How many noble natures, thought he, were there perishing for want of teaching! What but power like that of Him who said to the leper, " Be thou clean," could melt these hearts, hardened by the oppressor's wrongs, and taking their revenge in deeds of rapine and blood?

The good Bishop was oppressed by this thought, and by the consciousness of his

own insufficiency to effect that which he
felt was hardly less a miracle than that
of reviving the dead. What language
could he use to awaken the sympathy of
such an audience? — the most eloquent
words would be no better than a tinkling
cymbal to ears unused to any but the
harsh accents of violence and strife.

Ignatios felt, also, that strange sensation of awe, which men, even the most
accustomed to speak in public, have owned
to, when rising to address an assembly of
their fellow-men amid breathless silence;
they have felt their hearts knock against
their ribs, their lips quiver, and their
knees shake, before giving utterance to a
word.

So felt Ignatios at that moment: — the
very intenseness of his anxiety that his
first words should be words spoken in
season, chained his tongue, while Samuel,
who, with the Proto-palikari, had remained
for a few minutes in earnest consultation
behind the rest, outside the cave, strode

hastily forward, and taking his stand at
the opposite end of the altar, put an end
to the embarrassing silence, by bursting
forth into a chant of Δόξα τῷ Πατρὶ—
Gloria Patri, with a deep bass, the echoes
of which, reverberating through all the
aisles of the mountain cathedral, produced
the effect of a full choir. The example
once given, was followed by the Klephts.
Lawless as their mode of life now was,
there were among them those who, in
their boyish days, had been trained to
the services of their church, in whose
hearts even now there was still one chord,
slender though it might be, yet unbroken,
which only waited the wizard touch of
some early association to return harmo-
nious sounds of purer feeling.

There intervened a short pause, during
which the Bishop, having withdrawn from
his bosom his Doxasticon, gave forth that
thrilling verse of the glorious Ascension
Psalm,—" Who shall ascend into the hill

of the Lord? or who shall rise up in His
holy place?"

Samuel again led the chant, which was
immediately followed by all that strange
congregation, and now joined in by Angelica, in tones at first so timid and so low
as to be undistinguished in the midst of
the deeper and louder chorus of the men;
but by degrees, absorbed in her feelings
of devotion, and forgetting all other objects around her, as her heart, lifted up
like the everlasting doors, to let the
King of Glory come in, exulted in the
prospect of the Invisible and the Immortal, the tones of her voice gushed from
her inmost soul, so pure, so clear, so
heavenly-sweet, that, like the mountain
stream, which still retains its crystal freshness by the side of the turbid waters of
the plain, it rose distinct and clear above
the rest, soaring like the lark to the
gates of heaven, and so entranced the
attention of the rough men, that they,

one by one, ceased their singing, to listen to hers.

Angelica, for an instant unconscious of the stop, went on alone for a few notes, when, alarmed at the solitude of her voice, she abruptly ceased, and overpowered by the thousand conflicting emotions that seized upon her poor suffering heart, as it fell back to earth from the third heaven, she covered her face with her hands; and the only sound that now brake the silence which ensued was the voice of her weeping.

The Klephts held their breath, as if in respectful sympathy with her sorrows; while Ignatios, advancing to the front of the altar, and stretching forth his hand to demand their attention, began :—

" Παιδιάμου — My children, you have heard of David the shepherd; how, before he was raised to the throne of Israel, he lived as an outlaw, in caves and deserts, fleeing from one hiding-place to another, to avoid the persecution of his master

Saul. He it is who asks the question, 'Who shall ascend into the hill of the Lord? or who shall rise up in His holy place?'—and it is he who answers that question, thus:—'Even he that hath clean hands, and a pure heart.'

" My children, is there one among you who can dare look up to the King of Glory ascended, as on this day, into heaven, and say, ' *I* have clean hands, and a pure heart?' or rather, must not every one, with tears of repentance, cast himself down on the ground, and clinging to the cross of his crucified Saviour, cry, ' *Kyrie eleyson, Kyrie eleyson?*' "

The men's earnest looks, fixed upon the preacher, showed him that the question struck like a goad into their hearts.

While the Bishop yet spake, a vivid flash of lightning, instantly followed by a loud thunder-clap, illuminated the furthest recesses of the cavern. When the echoes had ceased, there was a moment of deep and solemn silence. Suddenly a groan was heard, more startling than the thunder. It was one of those hoarse groans, which seem to be torn up from the lowest depths of the remorseful conscience, such as may be fancied to give a half-stifled utterance to the despair of the damned. All eyes were turned in the direction of Yanko. It smote upon the heart of Angelica, with a distinctness of meaning of the unimaginable wretchedness it betrayed, which made her forget her own wrongs in the thought of her unworthy husband's misery. The very heinousness of his avowed crimes in the sight of offended Heaven, while it filled her with horror, excited her deepest compassion for his lost condition.

At that groan she rose hastily from her knees, and with the instinctive tenderness of her womanly heart moved towards the unhappy man. She had been hitherto concealed from observation by the altar, behind which she had placed herself. The eyes of all the Klephts, who still remained kneeling, were now turned upon her. As they gazed, and all but worshipped, they could see the rushing of the blood across that modest brow, turning its paleness into a roseate blush, like that which gives a transient warmth to the Alpine snows when confronted to the setting sun.

Angelica, painfully conscious of being the observed of all observers, hesitated whether to advance the step further which would bring her whole figure into their full view. One alone of all the Klephts was standing erect, at a short distance behind the rest; and as she raised her eyes to catch a cheering glimpse of the light of heaven beyond the cavern's mouth, they encountered the audacious look of the man from whose pursuit she had lately fled. That look terrified her; but it determined her onward movement to her husband's side.

" That is thy post, there thou must now stand or fall," was the inward prompting of her rigid sense of duty.

Like an angel on an errand of mercy and forgiveness, she approached him; but, as if he had seen the Avenger coming to seize his prey, he, with his face averted, and with his arms convulsively extended, exclaimed, with a maniac's scream,—" Touch me not!—begone!"

At the instant Angelica came within his reach, a pistol-shot resounded through the cavern. She staggered, and sank to the ground at the side of the altar.

The whole band arose in tumult, and there was a universal cry—"Away with him! kill him! He has lived too long! kill him! kill him!"

CHAPTER XLV.

" IT was not *he*. He has not *this* to answer for," were the first words which came from Angelica's lips, when, after a moment of bewildering confusion, caused by the suddenness of the . blow that had struck her to the ground, she became conscious of the meaning of those cries of vengeance.

To Ignatios and Photo, whom she perceived kneeling on either side, and leaning over her with looks of unspeakable anguish, she said—" Do not grieve for me, I shall soon be at rest. Let *him* only have time to repent. Pray for him— say that I forgive him all."

Observing blood mingled with the tears that were streaming down Photo's cheeks, she said,—"Thou, too, art wounded, Photo."

The bullet had slightly grazed his face as it sped on its fatal way to Angelica's bosom.

"It is nothing," answered Photo. "Would that my heart had been reached first."

"No; it is better so, my brother."

Angelica pressed her hand to her breast, as if trying to arrest for a few moments the ebbing of the life-stream.

She withdrew from her bosom a small packet, which dropped from her fingers, now too feeble to do their office; and looking into Photo's face, slowly and faintly said to him—"Take this; it belonged to my other brother. Wear it for his sake and mine."

She essayed to speak again, turning her eyes towards the Bishop. He rather divined, from the slight movement of her lips, than distinctly heard with his ears, the words "Forgive"—"*Sotirimou.*"

The lips ceased to move. The eyes, raised upwards, shone for an instant with a supernatural brightness, as if they had caught a ray from the heavenly glory, when the veil was drawn aside to let the released spirit pass into the unseen world.

A moment more, and that transient brightness was gone. The death-struggle was over. The good fight was fought. The shadows of Time had vanished into the realities of Eternity ; and she, whom those loving hearts were mourning as dead, was now among the truly living.

There lay before them that lovely form, a rigid corpse, calm, silent, impassive to the fearful strife that was raging close at hand.

Hardly was there time to remove the body out of sight to the back of the altar, and cast over it the veil and mantle worn by Angelica, when Samuel, who, with the Bishop and Photo, was hastily occupied in the sad office, was called away by piteous cries for help from Yanko. The

Klephts had rushed upon him like a pack of famished wolves, and the Butcher Palikari, foremost in the assault, was dragging him from his hiding corner, when the old Papàs, forcing his way through the crowd, succeeded in interposing his Anak stature between the assailants and their prey; and then, with uplifted arm and voice, having arrested the attention of all, he looked round the assembly with a scrutinizing glance, counting as he looked, and then spoke:—

" You are not all here, Palikaria— there is one missing. Were *he* present, he could tell who it was that fired that fatal shot, and why.

" As for *this* man," indicating with a gesture Yanko, who crouched behind him, " he has crimes enough to answer for, without adding to the number the murder of his wife. For them he deserves to die, but not by the hands of brave men like you. His hour is not yet come. We engaged, as you all know, to let him

go, on getting back from the hands of the
Toshki, Lambro Tzavella's son. Well,
him we have safe in our custody, thanks
to our good Bishop. We must now perform our part, and be true to our word.
We must redeem the Bishop's pledge
given to Alỳ Pasha on the faith of that
word, and let our hostage go free."

At this a confused murmur of dissen-
tient voices arose from the audience, in
which was distinguished above the rest,
like the hoarse croak of a carrion crow,
the voice of the Butcher,—" Are we to
let that fellow go free, after all the trouble
we have had with him?—No, no, he must
die the death. What's the Bishop's pledge
to us?"

Ignatios, who was sadly engaged in
watching by the stiffening remains of
Angelica, and absorbed in deep prayer,
hearing himself referred to in angry tones
that promised no friendly issue to the discussion, raised by Samuel's speech to the
Klephtourià, rose from his knees, and

appeared standing at his station by the altar.

All eyes and ears were now turned towards the Bishop, and the murmurs were succeeded by a respectful silence.

" Let the Bishop speak, and we will listen," exclaimed a friendly voice. It was that of the Suliote Dhimo.

Ignatios thus encouraged, in simple and dignified language then related what passed between himself and the Vezir, touching the exchange of the respective hostages. He described the manly bearing and invincible courage shown by the Suliote boy in all he had undergone during his captivity at Ioánnina, and dwelt particularly on the fortitude with which he had resisted the offers made him, if he would renounce his Christian faith and the cause of his fellow-countrymen. The Bishop concluded his narrative thus :—" You are many, παιδιάμου (my children), and I am only one. The decision of this matter rests with you. My

life is in your hands. You have heard
how I have pledged it to the Vezir. The
day of my return to Ioánnina without
Kyr Yanko or Photo Tzavella (one or
the other I bound myself to bring with
me), will be my last on earth. In such
matters, Alỳ Pasha is sure to keep his
word. If I am to lose my life in this
cause, let it be by friendly hands—by
yours, my own fellow-countrymen. My
son Photo will then be released from his
engagement; your brave leader, Papàs
Samuel, will be enabled to fulfil his towards Photo's sorrowing parents; and so,
if my life may not serve our common
country, my death at least may benefit
some one of our race."

" Bravely spoken !" exclaimed one of
the Klephts; " he is worthy to be a Klepht
himself!"

Before Ignatios had ceased speaking
Photo was at his side.

A marvellous change had come over
his whole person and appearance. The

expression of his countenance, his manner, his gait, were altogether altered. The stripling seemed to have suddenly shot up into the man. As young plants are said to acquire a rapid and portentous growth after a thunder-storm, so had the storm of suffering and sorrow, through which he had lately past, given Photo that insight into the depths of human woe, which, darkening all the hopeful visions of life, matured and fortified his spirit more than the lessons of a long experience could have done. While the tumult had been raging near, Photo had sat silent and apart, contemplating Angelica's features, calm and serene in the security of Death. There still lingered about her lips a celestial smile, as of a sleeping infant overshadowed by an angel's wing. All expression of pain and sorrow had fled. As he gazed, and felt the soothing influence of that solemn sight, he almost doubted whether a thing still so lovely was but a senseless corpse.

He took from his bosom the token of

remembrance which she gave him, devoutly kissed it, and unfolded the packet, fragrant with the perfume of violets, of which a leaf adhered to it, reddened with a drop of blood.

It was a small purse or pocket-book, beautifully embroidered in gold thread and seed pearl, with a cypher (Σ) worked on the outside, attached to a chain made of hair and silk intertwined.

The purse contained a paper, in which was a lock of hair, carefully fastened with a silk thread, and inscribed, "The last memorial of my beloved brother, Sotiri." There was another paper, on which were written, in most minute and beautifully delicate characters, several texts of holy Scripture, so disposed as to form the shape of a Greek cross. The text which served for the pedestal, on which the cross was made to rest, was in capital letters. It was this,—ΠΑΝΤΑ ΙΣΧΥΩ ΕΝ ΤΩ ΕΝΔΥΝΑΜΟΥΝΤΙ ΜΕ ΧΡΙΣΤΩ.*

* Philip. iv. 13.

The other texts were all preceptive of holiness, and exhorting to perseverance in faith and obedience; and in the corner was written, in the same delicate hand,— "The favourite texts taught me and Sotiri by my dear father. Blessed be their memories. The righteous shall be had in everlasting remembrance. Κυριε ελεησον."

The brave words of exhortation he had heard so lately proceeding from those lips came back to his heart's memory with redoubled force, and a deeper meaning, as he replaced the precious talisman in his bosom, saying to himself,—

"Thence shalt thou never part, but with my life's blood."

The flame of a pure and lofty resolution to devote henceforth that life to whatsoever things are true, honest, just, lovely, and of good report, was enkindled in that young and noble heart, never to be extinguished, and the young Suliote rose from the contemplation of the dead a living, earnest, and thoughtful man.

There was something in the serious and determined expression of Photo's dark eye which marked the inward change, as, in the presence of the whole assembly, after kneeling before the Bishop and respectfully kissing his hand, he rose to his full height, and then addressed him in a tone in which modesty and firmness were singularly and gracefully combined.

" O Dhéspota! To you I owe more than life—to you I owe the contempt of death. Shall I now forfeit the pledge I gave you? Think you I would shrink from its fulfilment when your life is at stake—yours, who have been more than a father to me? No, no. Decide what others may, *my* word shall not be falsified. Fain would I die fighting by the side of brave men against the vile Turks, but rather than Alý should have a pretext to injure a hair of your head, I will consent to rot in the dungeon from which I have escaped by your joint aid."

Photo turned to Samuel, who kissed the boy's forehead, and said, —

"Thou art a brave and truthful youth, Photakimou, and worthy to lead free men. Thou shalt *not* be again the prisoner of the Turk; nor shall our noble Bishop incur the hazard thou fearest.

"To be free, you must begin by being true," continued the old man, now addressing himself to the whole band. "Remember, Palikaria, you gave your word that this hostage of yours should be set at liberty on the release of Lambro Tzavella's son. Him you now see before you; and so the matter is settled."

A murmur of dissent was heard from a small knot, in which the Butcher and the ancient unwashed Palikari were pre-eminent.

Samuel affected not to hear it, and proceeded. "But before we set out to the succour of our brothers of Suli, who, you know, are anxiously expecting our arrival, there is a duty to be fulfilled, in

which you must lend me your assistance."

He pointed to the spot where lay the
body of Angelica.

" *That* must not be left here to be torn
to pieces by jackals and vultures. Which
of you, *paidhià*, will assist in conveying
those precious remains to the water's
side ? "

" All, all ! " was the answer unani-
mously returned to the appeal by which
Samuel quelled the outbreak of another
angry tumult.

After a short discussion it was arranged, that whilst the main body of the
Klephts set out on their march to the
appointed rendezvous, a few should remain to be the bearers of the corpse; for
which purpose a rude litter, made of
branches intertwined, and lined with fern
and moss, was hastily prepared.

But before they quitted the grotto
where all this scene had passed, many
went and knelt before the Bishop, kissed

his hand, and craved his blessing, and turned aside to take one glimpse at the beauteous dead.

There now remained in the cave none but the two ecclesiastics and the two redeemed hostages.

Yanko, the widower, sullen, stupified, motionless, seated on the ground, and staring on vacancy, was insensible to all around him. The terrors from within and from without seemed to have turned him, body and soul, into stone. The gentle Bishop would have addressed words of sympathy to the unhappy man. He wished to consult his wishes respecting the disposal of those precious remains, but he might as well have spoken to the rocks; they, at least, would have echoed back his words. He heeded not.

Ignatios determined in his own mind what he would do; he would himself accompany the body to his own church at Arta, perform the funeral rites, and see it deposited in the grave next the tomb destined for himself. Thus, at least, he could testify his affectionate remembrance of his much-loved friend Agathopoulo, while he showed respect for the virtues of his friend's ill-fated daughter.

The Klephts who had been selected for the office of bearers, and had meanwhile been employed in the construction of the litter to serve as the bier, now returned, and with the assistance of Samuel and Dhimo placed the body upon it.

It was truly a strange sight to observe with what careful tenderness those young men fulfilled their sad office. The face was left uncovered, after the Greek fashion, and the holy purity of its expression, which death itself could not efface, while it rebuked all light and dishonest imaginations, seemed to awaken in those wild outlaws thoughts, however transient, of higher and better things than was their wont.

"Now, my children," said Samuel, when all was arranged, " bear on, and get on as quick as possible to the boat that is waiting at the water-side. The day is wearing — the sky threatens — the Kyr Dhespotés will hardly have more day-light than enough to reach Salahora.

With sad and serious looks the bearers silently lifted the burden to their shoulders; and preceded by those who were to relieve them, and who carried their comrades' arms in addition to their own, the funeral procession was in a few moments winding its way down the steep and woody glen.

Yanko, roused from his torpor by Samuel, was made to take his place as chief mourner immediately after the bier, while the Bishop, leaning on Photo, followed.

CHAPTER XLVI.

SAMUEL, accompanied by Dhimo, took
a path that led by a shorter cut to the
sea-beach. On the way he informed him
more fully of the arrangements he had
made on the other side of the gulf, to
expedite the passage of the Klephtic
band across the interval which separated
them from the district of Suli. He indicated the rendezvous where he himself
would join them.

" To make all sure," said he, " I must
run the risk of crossing to Salahora, to
ascertain that nothing has been neglected
which can secure the success of our enter-
prise, while you, Dhimo, conduct the
march of the Palikaria till we join company. Do you keep Tzavella's son by
your side, and have an eye upon that mad

fellow. You know whom I mean. The bullet that deprived the woman of life was meant for that brave boy. Of this I doubt not, nor that it was that wretch who shot her. Watch him, and should you suspect him of an attempt against Photo, do not scruple to shoot him through the head, or cut him down without mercy, and let the Palikaria know I bid you do so."

" Trust me for that," replied the Suliote. " It will be no loss to be rid of such as he. I always suspected the fellow to be a coward, and his action has proved him so."

A few minutes brought them down to the water's edge. It was a narrow cove overshadowed by woods, of which the inlet was concealed by the jutting out of a low promontory, also thickly covered with trees, behind which the waters slept unruffled by the winds without. A boat lay there, fastened by a rope to the stem of a luxuriant arbutus, whose roots dipped into the water, slightly rocking to the ripple of the tiny wave which noiselessly kissed the shore.

The greeting which took place between Samuel and the weather-beaten, rough old seaman, who advanced to meet the Papàs, showed that they were not unknown to each other.

"I have been looking out for you some time," said Vasili. "One of your party was down here an hour ago, and I thought all the rest would have been here before now."

"Did you speak to the man?" said Samuel. "Did he say that we were coming?"

"I could not get a word out of him," replied Vasili: "the man looked half mad; and only muttered something to himself as he turned away through the woods over the cliff!"

Samuel looked at Dhimo, who replied by a nod of assent to the thought which the look signified.

The Palikaria who preceded the funeral

procession now appeared in sight, and soon after, while Samuel explained to the old boatman what was the sad freight his vessel was to receive on board, the whole party arrived, and the litter bearing the dead body of Angelica was deposited on the narrow beach. The face was covered with wild flowers and branches of fresh fern, to screen it from the sun's rays and the forest flies. That covering was now removed, and as the young men stood round the bier and gazed in mournful silence, the Bishop knelt down and prayed aloud. Photo knelt by him, and the rest followed his example. A few broken words of supplication for mercy and guidance were all that Ignatios could utter. With difficulty he could refrain from weeping as he fell on the young Suliote's neck and whispered his blessing.

Photo could not speak. He was for a moment unmanned by that sense of utter loneliness, which the bravest loving hearts feel most at the bitter instant of parting.

Samuel had stood aloof, the silent witness of the scene. He saw it was now time to interpose, to rouse the boy from the grief which threatened to overwhelm, as a flood, all his high and manly resolves.

He stepped forward and snatched Photo from the Bishop's embrace.

As Photo rose from his knees he turned to cast a last look on the dead, but the old priest hurried him away from the spot, and it was in a tone of almost stern rebuke that he said : " Son of Tzavella, enough of this. The living have other duties to fulfil than to sorrow needlessly for the dead. Now heed what I say. By to-morrow's sun thou may'st have to fight thy way through a host of Turks to thy father's house. Dhimo will tell thee of our plans—keep at his side during the march, till I join you again. And, mark me, beware of that——"

Before Samuel could complete the sentence, a ball came singing through the air, and passed so close to Photo's head as to make him wince. The colour came into his cheek as he looked up, as if ashamed of the momentary shrinking.

"My warning was not too soon," said Samuel. "That shot was meant for thee, child."

"And I will revenge it," replied Photo. "'T is he, Angelica's murderer — I see him yonder, hiding among the trees." And Photo was rushing up the steep bank to grapple with his foe, when Samuel pulled him back.

"Stand aside, I'll deal with that madman. Reserve thy courage for a worthier cause. Wait here for Dhimo and the Palikaria, and when they are come up bid them go on, and do thou go with them."

Photo would have followed Samuel, but the old man repeated his command with so peremptory a gesture, that he dared not disobey.

In a few giant strides, the priest had gained the summit of the promontory, on the edge of which, overhanging the sea, in a narrow space, clear of the trees which crowned it, was standing the profligate assassin. The mark of Cain was upon him, for there was that in his lowering and desperate look which showed the conscious wilful murderer.

Samuel, as he first caught sight of his features, exclaimed aloud, " 'T is the same."

" Yes," fiercely retorted the Klepht, "it is the same. 'T is I, whom thou, accursed priest! didst balk of my revenge. *She,* at least, is dead, and that is something. Had the last shot reached *his* heart I had died content."

So saying, the miserable man turned away, tossed up his arms, and at one spring plunged into the sea beneath.

" Wretched youth !" exclaimed Samuel, as he looked over the edge of the cliff down upon the water.

There was nothing to be seen of the frenzied imitator of Sappho's leap but a skull-cap floating above a sunken rock, against which he had dashed himself, and a slight tinge of blood on the wave.

" Had that blood been bravely shed in fighting against the Turk," was Samuel's soliloquy, as he hastened back to the boat, " well——but *thus!* how cowardly!"

So perished the self-destroyed victim of a frantic passion, which, under the sacred name of love, disguising the most un-principled selfishness, transforms man into a brute beast.

In the meanwhile the corpse had been put on board. Yanko had, unobserved, slunk away and stowed himself, as far as he could, out of sight, in the bows of the boat. The Bishop took his seat astern. Vasili awaited the return of Papàs Samuel to shove off. He was no sooner on board than each seized an oar, and in a few moments the vessel had rounded the point, and was in the open waters of the Ambracian Gulf.

The sun had passed the meridian. The

sky above was without a cloud. The atmosphere, unruffled and unrefreshed by the slightest breath of wind, glowed as with the white heat of a furnace. The motionless sea glared like a burnished mirror, with intolerable light.

The profound, death-like stillness of that lurid, stifling calm, was rendered more oppressive to the passengers in that solitary skiff, by being so sadly in unison with the solemn repose of the lifeless form which lay shrouded at their feet.

The dead body of an immortal being is an awful sight. A fearful thing it is to feel one's self alone in the silent, darkened chamber, from which the flaring light of day is shut out, and to gaze by the dim ray of a solitary taper upon the cold, senseless corpse, from which, as from its prison-house, hath so lately fled the undying spirit, unseen, unheard, unfelt by mortal sense. Yet there is in the very stillness and dimness of that spectacle something congenial with the great mys-

tery of death, which soothes while it
solemnizes the thoughts of the believing
mourner. But in the same spectacle,
seen in broad daylight, under the flashing
sunbeam, and in the open air, there
is something so unexpected, so clashing
with one's common, trivial, world-occu-
pied thoughts, that it would hardly be
more startling to meet face to face with a
sheeted ghost in the throng of the streets
or in the busy market. The only sound
that broke the still silence was that of the
creaking of the oars against the side of
the boat, and the gentle dip in the
smooth, unruffled water. The two rowers,
standing up, bending forward, each over
his single heavy oar, and looking a-head
of the vessel, seemed as if afraid by too
strenuous a motion to wake the dead.

They had advanced but a few strokes,
and were still close in with the shore, just
clear of some broken rocks that jutted
out from the base of the Lover's Leap,
when Vasili's oar striking against some-

thing which yielded to the stroke, he looked over the side, and exclaimed, as he turned his head back towards the Papàs,—"There's a drowned man!"

Samuel, by a significant look and gesture, bid him be silent. But the sudden exclamation aroused Yanko from his torpor, and broke in upon the meditations of the Bishop, which were leading him far away from the visible sadness at his feet, to the unseen glories of the world beyond the skies.

Yanko looked over the side of the boat, impelled by curiosity, to see the features of the drowned man.

" 'Tis no one you care for," said Samuel. " It is not Tzavella's son. It is only that miserable man, who, because he failed to shoot the boy, rushed down into the water, coward as he was, like the swine possessed by the devilish legion."

Yanko slunk back into the bottom of the boat. Samuel had accurately guessed his disappointment on finding that the drowned man was not Photo.

When, after rowing some time longer, they got fairly out into the broad gulf, a slight cat's-paw wrinkling the surface of the water gave hopes of a coming breeze, which made Vasili lay in his oar, and have all ready to hoist the sail. But there was as yet no wind to fill it, and the two old men went rowing on in silence. At last, the muttering of distant thunder was heard.

"We shall have wind enough by and by," said Vasili, as he turned an anxious eye to seaward.

"And more than enough, I warrant you," replied Samuel, who had laid in his oar, and seized the rudder. "Look how the sea is whitening yonder! Hark! it's coming on like a hurricane!"

Presently a sudden flash of forked lightning glittered from the dark purple arch of clouds, which had meanwhile rapidly encroached upon the clear blue vault of heaven, and after the pause of a few seconds, a sharp crack of thunder gave warning of the approaching strife above. It was like the signal-gun shot at the beginning of a great battle, the solemn herald of death to the thousands of fellow-men whom it invites to the slaughter of each other. The thunder-clap was succeeded by an interval of sepulchral stillness, during which the black clouds, heaped into dense, terrific masses, had so blotted out the light of the declining day, that it appeared as if night had already come.

Then came a second flash, of appalling splendour, which seemed to open a view into the very depths of the remote heavens, lighting up the wild sea and the surrounding coasts, and for one brief instant rendering vividly visible to each other the countenance and attitude of the tenants of that frail bark.

The next instant they were all plunged into utter darkness. It was like the appa-

rition of so many spectres. The dead
appeared to be living, for the heaving of
the boat, when struck by the surging
wave at the moment of the lightning's
flash, causing the senseless corpse to sway
from its supine posture, it seemed to be
suddenly endued with life, and a secret
undefinable horror crept along the veins
of one of the passengers, expecting at the
next flash to see that form sitting by his
side, no longer tenanted by the innocent
spirit which he had so cruelly outraged,
but now, for aught he knew, become the
habitation of some foul demon, sent before
the time to torment his guilty soul.

The shriek of terror which burst from
Yanko was lost in the crash of thunder
which now began to roll incessantly in
deafening peals, while the sea, lashed
into fury by the wolfish winds, tossed the
boat fearfully, threatening at every moment
to overwhelm it in the boiling waves.

In the midst of the elemental strife
the Bishop remained calm and unmoved,

as one whose house was built upon the rock. His was that prayerful attitude of soul, which, surrounded on every side by the most appalling dangers, has inspired believers in all ages with the heroic confidence that can say and feel, "Though the mountains be carried into the midst of the sea, yet shall not my heart be afraid."

The Papàs proved a good steersman, and gallantly maintained his station at the helm; the safety of all, indeed, mainly depended on his skill, and the strength of his arms, to obey the old boatman's instruction to keep the head to the wind. The irruption of one broad wave over her side must inevitably have swamped her.

" Praise be to Heaven and to St. Nicolas!" exclaimed Vasili, as he looked to windward; "'tis clearing up there: the sea is going down, the storm is passing off towards the mountains: we shall have the wind fair in a few minutes."

It was not long before the old boatman's

weather-wise anticipations were realised. As the storm passed away, and only a few mutterings of thunder continued to be occasionally heard in the distance, like the last volleys of the rear-guard of a retreating army, the line of coast towards which they were bound became faintly visible by the reflection of the blood-red streak along the western horizon, where the sun had sunk in gloomy grandeur.

"The breeze is now right aft," said Vasili. "If you, O Papàs, will look to the sail, I will take the helm, for we shall soon be nearing the land."

At the end of half-an-hour's prosperous navigation the boat touched the shore, and before there was time to disembark the voice of a man, whose figure, dimly seen standing on the beach, loomed like a calpacked Tatàr, was heard to exclaim, "Hallo! Carabochiere, is Kyr Nikóla in that boat?"

Another voice followed with the question,—"Is the Bishop there, too?"

"Both are here," answered Vasili.

Ignatios recognised the voice of his own Palikari, Yorgi, and that of Emin Aga, the Vezir's Tatàr, who had escorted him from Ioánnina, but had prudently eschewed the risk of crossing the water, and of trusting himself to the tender mercies of the Klephts.

Presently other figures were descried coming down to the margin of the water, to whom Vasili called in the familiar tone of one who felt himself at home among friends and neighbours.

"Children, come down, some of you, and give us a helping hand to land our——"

The old man hesitated how he should finish the sentence—adding in an undertone,—

"Kyr Nikóla, you must be so good as to explain it all, and give your directions as to what is to be done about the ——"

Vasili raised his voice again—"We must have a lantern or two to give us light, and a plank for the Kyr Dhespotés and the Effendi."

A voice from the group answered,— "Spiraki is coming down with a light: he'll be here presently."

At the mention of Spiraki's name, Samuel, without saying a word to anybody, dropped himself out of the boat into the water, and passing behind the people, so as to escape observation, hurried towards the cottage from which the promised light was at that moment seen to issue.

Samuel, as he approached, said in a low voice,—"Spiraki."

" Εγω ειμι—It is I," replied the young fisherman, and was about raising the lantern to the face of the speaker, when the old Papàs struck it out of his hand, saying,—

"It is I, Samuel,—Is all arranged as we agreed?"

"Everything is done as you wished," said Spiraki. "The cattle will be all at the place before the moon's up, and you may depend upon the men."

"That's right! Well, now listen and do what I tell you. That cursed Vlackh is in the boat with his wife's dead body. The Tatàr is waiting for him on the beach. They must both be detained here till to-morrow morning, or he will be giving information that may ruin our plans. I trust to your wit, Spiraki, to contrive that, for I must be off at once to meet the Palikaria at our rendezvous. It will be as much as I can do to get there in time."

Spiraki, while Samuel was speaking, had taken him by the hand, and led him to the back of the cottage.

"The Menzil is close by," said he; "the horses are all saddled, and ready to start. There is not a soul there now. Everybody, Surejees and all, are gone down to the boat. Come with me. As for Emin Aga, don't fear his being be-forehand with you. He is half-drunk already, and I'll take care to put another flask of rackee in his reach, that will set him asleep for the rest of the night."

By this time they had reached the stable. Spiraki helped the old Papàs to mount the first horse he came to; it happened to be the Surejee's.

" These *irrationals** know the road, in pitch dark as well as in broad daylight," observed Spiraki, as he led the horse out of the stable-yard. The other horses, accustomed to follow, followed as a matter of course.

" They will stop of themselves at the bridge; God speed you!"

In a moment the whole cavalry of the station was full gallop on the road leading to Arta, headed by the brave old Caloyero, who was as much at home in the saddle as in a boat.

When Spiraki, having relighted his lantern, ran down to the beach, he was

* Ἄλογα, the modern Greek for horses.

greeted with exclamations of abuse and impatience for having kept everybody waiting so long.

" Τί νά κάμω;—What can I do?" answered he, in the tone of an injured innocent; "how could I help the wind blowing the candle out? What can a man do?"

" Never mind what a man can do or can't do," said Vasili; " but now you have lighted your candle, just help us to see what we are about."

A' sad sight was then revealed to the eyes of the beholders as the flickering light fell upon the corpse. Over the rigid limbs, which, from the rough handling of the storm, were partially exposed to view, the old fisherman hastily threw the sail, with that natural instinct which prompts the living to respect the helpless dead.

The spectators silently looked at each other with wonder and anxious curiosity, doubting what this mean$_t$; and as the light fell upon the face of Ignatios, who waited the removal of the body before leaving his seat, a whisper passed from one to the other — " It is the Lord Bishop."

A few words, meanwhile, passed between him and Vasili, with respect to the disposal of the body for that night; and it was agreed that it should be conveyed to the old man's cottage, where he said " his old wife, who was as good as any Kalógrya,* and better than most of them," would see that everything was arranged as it should be.

While the landing of that sad freight was being effected, Spiraki was sent forward to bid his mother prepare for its reception.

It was only when the men, bearing the body on their shoulders, were departed, and the beach was cleared of all except

* A nun: literally, a good old woman.

Yorgi and the Tatàr, that Yanko ventured to leave the boat.

He was accosted by the latter with a huskiness of voice that betrayed his recent violation of the Prophet's prohibition against intoxicating drink.

"Welcome, Kyr Nikóla! I am glad to see you safe back again. A man's life is not worth the crack of a whip that falls into the clutches of those children of the devil. You may thank your Kismet to have escaped with no greater loss than your ears. Come on with me to the Menzil—all is ready for our journey. The Vezir is impatient to see you."

Yanko was in no condition to say yea or nay to the Turk's command. He followed him mechanically, without turning to say a word to the Bishop, who, overwhelmed with fatigue of mind and body, proceeded, under Yorgi's guidance, to the lodging provided for him in the hamlet. But Yanko was spared the night journey in his then pitiable plight, by the contrivance, as we have seen, of the young fisherman, who, moreover, contrived effectually to lay an embargo on the Tatàr by putting in his way the irresistible temptation of a bottle of the strongest rackee.

CHAPTER XLVII.

THE next morning's sun, which rose in a sky transparently bright, like a polished floor of crystal and lapis lazuli, swept clean by the storms of the preceding night, gave light and life to the dark narrow streets of the town of Arta, where lay in deep repose, after the fatigue and risks of a rapid flight from Ioánnina, Christodhoulo and Arghyrousa, forgetting in the sweets of the bridal honey the shrewd taste of the bitter almond, which had been their early lot.

The narration of that flight would form too long an episode to be allowed to interrupt our story at this critical juncture. Let the reader be content to know that Arghyrousa, under the safeguard of her idiot mask, contrived to escape out of the

Vezir's harem, and that with the assistance, and under the guidance of the young
fisherman Spiraki, she and her husband,
following close upon the track of the
Bishop of Arta's party on its departure
from Ioánnina, reached Arta, and were
safely housed under the roof of a kins-
man's of their guide.

On that morning, the morrow of Ascension Day, the principal thoroughfare of
that ancient episcopal city was all alive
with the Greek portion of its inhabitants.
Men, women, and children, attired in
their best holiday apparel, were hastening
forth on the road leading to the port, so
to call it, of Salahora, and from the lively
tones of their merry voices and cheerful
looks it was evident that they were all
intent on some common object of re-
joicing.

"But is it quite certain that he is
really come back, and all safe and sound?"
said one to his companion.

"Not a doubt of it," replied the other.

" I saw somebody who saw the Dhespoté's groom, who said he knew that the
Palikári Yorghi — you know Yorghi —
was at Salahora last night."

" Well," said the first, " I never hoped
to see our good Bishop again, after I
heard of his having ventured among those
Klephts, and, all to ransom that——."
Here the speaker dropped his voice.

" Oh !" rejoined the other, " there's
not a Klepht, who has true Hellenic
blood in his veins, that would not give
every drop of it to save our Ignatios from
harm. Why, man, they all know he is
the real friend of our nation; and they, as
well as *we*, all have the same object — to
be rid of those asses of Turks. But as
for that Vlackh, who is as malicious as
he is ugly, I would not answer for *his*
thick head if it got within pistol-shot of
them."

A third interlocutor here put in a
word. " His thick head *has* escaped,
however ; for he landed last night with

the Bishop, and is now on the road with him."

"ΘαυμαϭΊο πϱαγμα!—Wonderful thing!" observed the other. "For such a pestilent fellow to have got away with a whole skin from the Klephts of Macrinoro, and to have escaped yesterday's storm, he must be reserved for some strange fate indeed. But how soon are they likely to be here?"

"Oh, not for two or three hours. There came over a dead body in the boat. I don't know who it is—people say it is Lambro Tzavella's son, who was killed by some accident, and that the Bishop brought the body here to secure it decent burial, rather than leave it a prey to the jackals."

"Poor lad! Well, there's one who will not shed tears at his funeral. The Vezir is in high luck to recover *his* jackal, and be rid of a brave Greek heart, who, had he lived, would have turned out the bravest of the brave."

This conversation, which took place in the street near the bazaar, was overheard and eagerly listened to by Christodhoulo, who, it will be remembered was the so-called Palikari of Kyr Yanko.

Christodhoulo had been roused up and sent forth by his wife, considerably against his will, to pick up what news were to be learnt in the bazaar, with the hope of obtaining some tidings of their mistress, Kyrà Angelica.

But he found the bazaar deserted. Every stall was shut up, and every creature gone, except a wretched cur or two prowling about in search of a bone, and one old Turk, the proprietor of a stall, who, indifferent to all the hubbub and excitement among his Guiaoor fellow-citizens, was squatted cross-legged on his shop-board, imperturbably smoking his tchibouk, supplied with tobacco from his own shop stores.

To extract any news from such a source was a hopeless task. So Christodhoulo returned to tell Arghyrousa what he had heard.

"'Εγλύτωσε!—Escaped!" was the first word he uttered as he entered the room, in which his wife still lay, hardly yet awake, upon the mattrass spread, *à la Turque*, upon the floor. The lamentable voice with which that single word was uttered did not betoken a satisfactional sympathy in the escape of the individual, whoever it might be; and Arghyrousa was too sleepy to express any curiosity or care about the matter.

"Δεν ηκουσες, μαλακιαμια;—Don't you hear, my dear?" said Christodhoulo, impatiently. "'Εγύρισεν ὅ ἐφένδης με τον δεσπότην—Master is come back with the Bishop."

Arghyrousa now sat bolt upright, wide awake.

"Καὶ ἡ κυρά;—And our mistress?" she exclaimed.

"I heard nothing of her," replied Christodhoulo hesitatingly, as a sudden misgiving shot across him. He caught it from the anxious look which accompanied his wife's question.

" Christodhoulo, you know more than you dare tell," said Arghyrousa, whose anxiety rose to alarm at his hesitation. " Tell me all you have heard."

Christodhoulo repeated faithfully the conversation he had overheard in the street.

" Poor Photaki! poor boy!" said Arghyrousa, and her eyes filled with tears.

" But what's become of my dear mistress? She can't have arrived in time! Where can she be now?"

Christodhoulo interposed: " That Dervish Papàs,—was he, after all, a sure man?"

" Oh, don't torture me with such horrible surmises! A sure man! Yes, I am sure he is. I would as soon mistrust him as you, Christaki."

But her faltering voice belied her profession of confidence, and a passionate flood of tears poured forth from the troubled depths of her heart, distracted by fear and suspicion.

"Have you heard nothing of Spiraki?" said she now, while she hastily arose and adjusted her dress. "He said he should be back again this morning."

"No," said Christodhoulo; "perhaps the people of the house can tell. I'll go and see."

He presently returned, and told his wife that Spiraki had just come in, leaving word that the Bishop was approaching the town, and that the people were crowding to the church, whither it was said he was proceeding for the funeral, but *whose* he did not say. Kyr Yanko, he added, accompanied the Bishop.

"Kyr Yanko at the funeral of that poor boy, whom he would have willingly seen rot in prison! The vile hypocrite!" said Arghyrousa. "And yet, what will his Pasha say when he hears of it? But let us go to the church at once, my Christaki; I wish to get there before it is filled with the crowd. Come, help me on with that veil. My poor dear mistress!—oh, where, where can she be? Perhaps the good Bishop—they say he is so kind and affable to all—will help us in our distress. I cannot endure this cruel suspense—it will kill me."

The house where they were lodged was not far from the church ; in a few minutes the couple reached the only entrance, then open, into the sacred edifice—a low and narrow door, so contrived that only one at a time could enter—a contrivance meant not so much to enforce a posture of humility on passing the threshold of the house of God, as to put an obstacle to the entrance of Turks on horseback, which had sometimes been attempted in Greek churches where such precautions had not been taken.

Arghyrousa, finding a place vacant on the women's side, not far from the catafalque, prepared for the reception of the bier during the funeral service, took her seat, and kneeling down, covered her face with her hands, and remained immersed in sad foreboding thoughts, heedless of the noise and bustle around her, which increased at every moment as the throng from without approached.

The principal door was now thrown open to admit the bier, which was carried aloft upon the shoulders of its six bearers, preceded by the priests, each holding a lighted taper, and whose pale ascetic features, and dark flowing robes, were in solemn harmony with the mournful rites they were engaged in.

Arghyrousa heard the heavy tramp of the feet of the bearers upon the surrounding pavement, as they moved with measured steps up the nave; and her throbbing heart beat time to their tread. When they stopped to deposit their sad burthen on the stand prepared to receive it, the pulses of her heart seemed to cease too, and an undefinable horror came over her, like that which sometimes seizes the midnight watcher, waiting in breathless dread the apparition of a ghost.

Sickened at heart with the suspense which a look would remove, yet not daring to lift up her eyes lest they should confirm its miserable misgivings, her agitation was for a moment suspended by the solemn chant of the priests.

When the chant had ceased, a death-like silence pervaded the assembly for a few moments; it was succeeded by the suppressed whispering of voices, when Arghyrousa caught the meaning from the words of those near her—"So young—so beautiful—so cruelly murdered!"

Was it of Photo they were speaking? or could it be Angelica?

After a short but solemn pause, the voice of the Bishop, who had taken his station in front of the altar, was heard pronouncing the solemnly affecting invitation which forms part of the burial service of the Greek Church, addressed to the mourners for the dead:—"Come, ye mourners, and give the last embrace to the dead, before she is removed for ever from your eyes."

Before the last word had passed the Bishop's lips, Arghyrousa had started from her knees, rushed to the bier in which lay, with uncovered face, her head crowned with a garland of fresh flowers, the dead Angelica. One bitter cry — a shriek that thrilled through every heart — and the faithful, affectionate, noble-hearted Arghyrousa, fell swooning upon that lifeless frame, her lips fastened upon the cold lips of her beloved mistress.

Christodhoulo had taken his place on the men's side, lower down the church, and not caring to be seen by his master Yanko before ascertaining in what temper he should find him, had turned his head away when the procession entered the church, (in which the widower followed most unwillingly), and had remained till now in the belief that it was the body of

Photo which lay in that bier. So when
he heard the cry of his wife, and saw her
fall upon the corpse, a sudden pang of
fiercest jealousy shot through his whole
frame, and he made his way towards her,
pushing through the crowd with the fury
of a madman, till, reaching the spot and
seeing that sad spectacle of unmitigable
woe, he stood stupified with horror; his
jealous rage in the instant melted into a
gush of feminine tenderness, intermingled
by a feeling of the keenest self-reproach;
and he sank upon his knees on the pavement at the foot of the bier, dissolved in
an agony of tears.

Arghyrousa, in the meanwhile, having
been withdrawn from the body, her veil
torn aside, her face sprinkled with water
suddenly snatched from the font, and with
such other appliances for her relief as were
suggested by the compassion of the women
nearest to her, she after a little space
began to recover from her swoon. At

first she looked listlessly around her, unconscious of the scene, like one awakening
out of a dream.

Presently her eyes became suddenly
arrested, and intently fixed upon one object in the surrounding throng. She
started upon her feet, pushed aside with
an imperious gesture those who had been
busied in assisting her, raised herself to
her full height, advanced towards the bier,
and with her right hand stretched out,
and following the direction of her flashing
eyes, she exclaimed, in a voice that
sounded preter-human,—"That is the
murderer!" All eyes were now fixed
upon the ashy face of Yanko, who stood,
pale and trembling, his knees knocking
against each other, his teeth chattering
with terror.

With her raven tresses all dishevelled,
and streaming down her shoulders and
across her bosom; with her disordered,
half-maddened looks, and distended nostrils, Arghyrousa might have passed for

the Pythian priestess at the shrine of
Delphi.

Yanko shrank from her awful glance.
He cast an imploring look towards Ignatios, who was standing at the altar, contemplating with pity the passion of the
poor distracted woman.

The Bishop advanced towards the bier.
" Daughter ——," he said.

She turned fiercely round upon him.
" Daughter!" she exclaimed; " who calls
me daughter? I have never known father
nor mother. *She* alone was everything
to me, and *he* has made me doubly an
orphan in murdering that angel."

As she spoke, her madly roving eye
met the calm look of the venerable man
fixed upon her, so meekly, so compassion-
ately, so sorrowfully! It was like a ray of
light breaking through the blackness of
the thunder-clouds. While it betokened
the deepest commiseration for her grief,
it seemed to rebuke the violence of her
passion.

" My daughter!" he repeated. That loving appellation, pronounced in an accent of exquisite sweetness, fell upon the ear of that poor sufferer " as the small rain upon the tender herb, and as the showers upon the grass." It penetrated through the scorched and withered surface of her desert heart, bringing back to life the gentler affections of her ardent nature, which the simoon of despair seemed to have suddenly overwhelmed and blasted for ever.

Her threatening attitude—her eye, erst glittering with the lurid light of incipient madness—the hollow, unnatural sound of her voice, which seemed to issue from the tomb,—all, all were changed, as, gazing upon those benign and placid features, with an expression in which a pleased surprise, and trust, and fear were strangely mingled, she sank down at the Bishop's feet, and wept aloud.

Her husband—he, too, knelt down by her side, supporting her, and whispering words of affection in her ear. The emotion was contagious; the women, who were near witnesses of this scene, began also to weep; and the sympathy, like the electric spark, pervading every link of the chain which binds together human hearts, the whole congregation was soon dissolved in tears; and sobs and sighs resounded through the church. One only remained untouched. Yanko stood motionless; his heart, from fear, was turned to stone. If he could then think at all, it was only to anticipate, from the indignation of all present, the vengeance due for the imputed murder of that lovely victim stretched out before their view. But there came to his relief an unexpected succour.

A loud and violent knocking was suddenly heard at the church door, which caused all to look up, and listen in suspense and alarm. An angry and impatient voice was heard outside, and the imprecation in common use among Moslems, applied with peculiar venom against all

Rayàhs and Guiaoors, was distinguished. All turned their eyes towards their Bishop, as if seeking guidance and courage from his glance.

The knocking outside was repeated with greater violence, and then the same voice, more angry and impatient still, prefaced with an untranslatable imprecation, pronounced these words:—

"Open!—a command from the Vezir!—open!"

All in the church shuddered at the sound — the women with terror, the men with suppressed indignation. One only, the Vezir's worthy agent, Yanko, inwardly smiled, — for he trusted his escape was secured. The Bishop preserved his presence of mind. He beckoned with his hand, and all waited for his word.

"Be still, my children; — take your accustomed places. I will go and receive the Vezir's messenger. Kyr Yanko, be pleased to come with me. The Vezir's commands probably concern you."

So saying, Ignatios walked with a firm step down to the nave, and ordered one of the bystanders, who happened to be Spiraki, the young fisherman, to unbolt the side-door.

On the door being thrown open, those in the church who stood in a line with it could perceive no more than the heavy boots and skirts of an express Tatàr's riding-habit, for the upper part of the wearer's person was kept out of sight by the well-calculated lowness of the narrow entrance, which compelled the bearer of the Pasha's commands to bow down his Moslem pride with a most unwilling humility. In doing so, the messenger did not calculate with mathematical precision the altitude of his kalpak, so that, making his dive with a momentum proportionate to his angry impatience, he emerged from the street into the church without his *couvre-chef*, and with a considerable increase of ill temper. At the same time, the huge yatagan which he carried in his girdle, slipped out and fell upon the mat, inside the door. The consciousness that the baldness of his pate, relieved only by the single top-lock, the handle by which he hoped to be hoisted into his Prophet's Paradise, was revealed to the sight of a congregation of Guiaoors and Rayàhs, added not a little to his exasperation. He thrust a paper, which he took out of his bosom, into the face of the Bishop, and with a most insolent gesture and peremptory tone, said,—

" *Bré Dhespoté!* — Here, you fellow, Bishop! take the master's buyurdèe — Read."

Having done so, the fellow looked round him with the self-sufficient air assumed by the slavish *employés* of autocrats, so long as they think themselves sure of impunity, and in a loud tone issued a general order that some one, designating the whole assembly by a contemptuous epithet, should fetch him his kalpak.

Nobody stirred. A general murmur of indignation was heard among the men, and the women crowded together, like doves at the sight of the hawk. To see their beloved Bishop accosted with such disrespect, and to hear themselves and their faith vilified by a brutal infidel, within the precincts of their own house of prayer, was more than they could bear, accustomed though they were to such treatment. Ignatios observed the swelling of the storm. He resumed his station at the altar, and all eyes were again fixed upon him, while he opened the paper and perused it in silence. The change in the usually calm expression of his countenance betrayed strong emotions of indignation and disgust. He remained silent for a moment. The motion of a butterfly's wing might have been heard in that throng; while the whole assembly stood up in breathless expectation of what that silence portended.

Ignatios handed the paper to Yanko, and said,—

" Kyr Nikóla, read this before it is made known to the assembly: to you, appeal will be made as to the truth of the facts on which the Vezir's commands are grounded."

Yanko read it, and turned yellow and green at its perusal. He returned it to the Bishop without saying a word.

" This command, my children, is addressed to your Bishop," said Ignatios. " I am required to use my diligence to trace to her hiding-place, to cause to be seized, and to secure in prison till His Highness's further pleasure shall be made known. Kyrà Angelica, the wife of Kyr Nikóla of Kalarýtes, accused of having, under a fraudulent pretext, found access into the seraï of Ioánnina, and having then stolen valuable jewels belonging to the Vezir, with which she afterwards decamped, and is supposed to have fled to Arta, with the intention of escaping by sea to Frenguià. And furthermore, she is accused of deserting her husband, from love of the Guiaoor, the Suliote Photo Tzavella, aiding and abetting the rebellious Rayàhs of Suli. The community of Arta to pay five hundred purses."

" Five hundred purses!" was the translation of the groan which was heard to issue from the treasury benches of the church, the usual seat of the elders and wealthy men of the community, when the perusal of the Vezirian ukase was completed.

A dead silence followed. Every one waited for the Bishop's comments on that document.

"Brethren, — You have heard the Vezir's buyurdèe. That His Highness has been misled by false reports, we have the proof under our own eyes. The body of the fugitive which we are required to secure, and cast into prison, is lying dead in that narrow coffin. But no prison can confine the immortal spirit : *that* has escaped beyond the reach of all human pursuit, and now abides, as we all must do, Sultans as well as Rayàhs, priests as well as people, the final sentence of our great Judge. If there be one who can stand on that day before the tribunal of the Son of man, and not be ashamed, it will be the pure and holy soul so lately fled from the prison of the flesh. You, Kyr Nikóla, can answer to the assembly here present, that your wife was not the woman to desert her husband in his need, for you know that it was in the fulfilment of her wifely duty, and by your express written order, that she presented herself before the Vezir, to procure the means of your liberation from captivity. She, as you know, fell a victim to her heroic devotion to that duty; and yet she is stigmatised in this paper as an adulteress and a thief! Thou, O God, knowest the secrets of all hearts!"

This appeal, pronounced with a deep,

earnest tone, thrilled through every heart.

There was an awful pause, till Ignatios, fixing his eyes full upon Yanko's downcast face, said, — "Kyr Nikóla, I call upon you, in presence of this assembly, and of the bearer of this the Vezir's command, to confirm the truth of what I have said, and to declare that the allegations on which that command is founded, and which are adduced as the grounds of imposing an *avania* on my people, are totally groundless. I adjure you, in the name of our common Saviour and Judge, and upon the holy Gospels, to declare that these allegations are utterly false."

At a motion of the Bishop, a deacon reached the book to Yanko, who, putting his hand upon it, bowed his head, and faintly said,—"I do."

At this, Arghyrousa, who had all this time been watching him with the eye of a lynx, suddenly exclaimed, "Then give her the parting kiss."

Yanko glanced at the woman with a bewildered and yet vengeful look, as if doubting what to do.

" See," she cried, " he hesitates! He *was* the murderer of my dearest mistress!"

Here the Tatàr, who, during all this scene had remained a phlegmatic spectator, stepped forward.

" Kyr Dhespotés, I have a word more to say by the Vezir's commands, which concerns the serving-maid of Kyr Nikóla's wife. That woman is she. She it was who aided in the escape, and, *Allah bilir!*— God knows,—has, no doubt, got the jewels. As the mistress is dead, the maid must answer for her. So, come along with me, woman, before the Musselìm; he shall examine into the matter. Come, come, I have no time to lose with you. Kyr Nikóla, my orders are to start immediately with you, to meet the Vezir by to-morrow morning at the tchiflik near Prevesa. The horses are all ready at the Menzil."

A snarl of diabolical satisfaction dilated the wooden features of Yanko at this diversion in his favour, which produced a correspondent consternation and alarm visible in the countenances of all around, especially of Christodhoulo, who, during the Tatàr's address, placed himself close by the side of his wife.

" The Vezir's buyurdèe says nothing of Kyrà Angelica's serving-maid," said the Bishop to the Tatàr. In a matter of such consequence His Highness would no doubt have mentioned it. Your quick return with Kyr Nikóla to the Vezir is of much greater consequence than this affair. I myself will write, and give the explanations which I am sure will satisfy His Highness on the matter."

" That is all *bosh lakerdì*—empty talk," replied the Tatàr. " My word is as good a warrant as the Vezir's buyurdèe." And he was going to seize Arghyrousa by the arm to drag her away, when her husband, whose blood by this time had got up to boiling heat, placed himself before her, and shrieked like an eagle defending his mate :—

"Touch my wife with but the tip of your finger, and I'll dash your head on this pavement!"

At the same moment the other men, thronging round, pressed and hustled the Turk so closely that it was impossible for him to move. At a motion from Ignatios, who was anxious to prevent violence which should give a pretext for an *avania*, Arghyrousa was made to glide away at the back of the crowd, and with her husband, and under the escort of Spiraki, left the church, and were soon out of sight. The streets being entirely deserted, they got away beyond the reach of present pursuit.

The Tatàr, finding himself powerless in the midst of enemies, now gave a sulky adhesion to the counsel of the Bishop, and left the church with Yanko, to go and prepare for their journey to meet the Vezir. The funeral service was then concluded, and the body conveyed to the cemetery amid the lamentations of all the people.

CHAPTER XLVIII.

FROM the moment Lambro Tzavella sent his famous letter of defiance to Alỳ Pasha, the Suliotes knew that they had nothing to expect from that crafty tyrant but war *to the knife*. They accordingly made up their minds to the worst, and set about their preparations for defence.

On the other hand, the renewed efforts which Alỳ now determined to make for their subjugation were stimulated by the apprehensions he, not unreasonably, entertained, lest the French commandant of Corfù should furnish his enemies with the means of successfully resisting his power.

He therefore lost not a moment, and spared no pains in his endeavours to penetrate the designs, and to obtain information with respect to the movements of his new neighbours in the Ionian Islands; at the same time that he gathered together numerous troops from the most warlike districts of his Pashalyk, and proceeded to take possession of the principal inlets into that mountain lair, with a view to cut off all supplies from the neighbouring country, and to starve the Suliotes into unconditional surrender.

It has been seen that the necessity of employing an experienced and confidential agent for the accomplishment of the first object, was the urgent motive which induced him to give up his Suliote hostage for the recovery of Yanko. And now such was Alý's impatience on that head, and his anxiety to ascertain what he had to fear from the French, aroused as his suspicions were by the sudden mission of that impromptu Extraordinary Envoy, Citizen Leonidas Tite Bouchon, that he decided to proceed himself to the neighbourhood of Prevesa, then a dependance of the Ionian Republic and in possession of the French, and appointed there his rendezvous with his Jackal and the Frenchman, as the most convenient spot whence to watch the movements of his enemies.

The investment of Suli by the Vezir's forces was not yet so complete as to intercept all communication through its territory between the coast and the inland country.

The usual traffic between Arta and the little town of Parga was still carried on, subject to the vexatious surveillance of the Vezir's officers, who had strict orders to see that it should not be used for the supply of provisions, and especially of arms and ammunition, to the Suliotes. But the surveillance was not so uniformly strict as not to be occasionally eluded, and sometimes outbribed; and it was by single foot-messengers, who found their way by by-paths across the almost inaccessible crags of the hills that looked down on every side upon the insulated rock of Trypa, that these mountaineers obtained intelligence of what was said and done—frequently, too, of what was *not* said and *not* done—beyond the boundaries of their little world.

One of these retailers of news had dropped, *en passant*, the report, rife at Arta, that the son of Lambro Tzavella had turned Turk at the moment of his being led out to execution at Ioánnina. The report before reaching Suli had, by the details which every one contributed *ad libitum* in its passages through many mouths of various capacity for the transmission or distortion of truth, swelled into the proportions of a gigantic lie. The terror of death, the allurement of an embroidered jacket, and the exhortations of a renegado, had been the ostensible motives of the youth's apostasy; but it was whispered, and affected to be believed by those who pretended to know more than the public in general, that the real cause of a conduct so unworthy of a Suliote was the desperate passion which he and Yanko's wife had conceived for each other, during his stay at Kalarýtes. It was added upon the same indubitable authority, that Madame had contrived the abduction of Monsieur by Klephts, with whom she was in league; and when rid of her husband, had lost no time in going to Ioánnina, and had there and then formally declared herself a *Mussulwoman* in the presence of the Cadi.

Had that report reached the ears of Photo's mother? Was there no kind friend or neighbour who, under pretence of comforting her, hastened to repeat the news, with the addition of one drop more of venom? No; a base act, perpetrated by a child of Suli, was felt and lamented as a disgrace and a calamity by the whole community. Mosco was the only one who had yet heard nothing.

Alas! for that poor fond mother!

Ever since the day Samuel had quitted
Suli, solemnly promising to bring back
her darling Photo, or perish in the attempt, she, treasuring up in her heart's
memory every syllable of that promise,
had resorted, morning and evening, to a
solitary spot on the mountain side, whence
she could descry every living thing that
moved in the dell beneath, from which a
stony path led to the level of the height
where she sat.

It was along that path that Mosco
expected from day to day to see the figure
of her child and his liberator appear.
Her eyes, frequently dim with tears, were
unceasingly strained in the same direction. If she took them off for a moment
to look to other points of her limited
horizon, it was only with a more intense
gaze that they returned and fixed themselves on a particular spot, where, at an
abrupt turn of the valley, the onward
path was excluded from her view by the
interposition of a mass of rock, all black

and shivered by the thunderbolts, or perhaps the earthquake, which had hurled
it down into the valley from the over-
toppling crags.

Poor, patient, watchful heart, that
beats only in a mother's bosom! Thou
that endurest so meekly, so silently,
even the neglect or the forgetfulness of
thy absent child, defending while others
reproach, excusing where others con-
demn, thou truly knowest what are
the pangs of hope long deferred, while
the daily renewal of bitter disappointment forces from thee, each morning, the
desponding cry, " Would God it were
even ! " and in the evening, " Would God
it were morning ! "

On the morning when the report respecting Tzavella's son was beginning to
be confidentially whispered in the ears of
particular friends, as a secret not to be
divulged to a living soul, it happened that
Mosco came down from her lonely watch-
tower to return to her childless abode. It

was about the time when the women usually assembled at the village fountain with their pitchers, to draw water for the supply of their respective households. The fountain was to them what the Agora was for the idlers of Athens,—the place where everybody was occupied in telling or hearing something new, and as it was frequented by the younger portion of the female community, on whom devolved the household duties, as the hewers of wood and drawers of water, there seldom was lack of noisy talk and merry laughter while they waited for their turn to fill their vessels. But now the usual sound of cheerful voices was not heard. The women were engaged in mournful and earnest talk, which abruptly ceased as one, the elder of the group, said, " Silence, *his* mother is coming."

As she passed by, with sad and down-cast eyes, the women watched her in silence, observing how pale and careworn she looked, and sighed to think to what

greater misery that wretched mother's
heart was doomed, when the report of her
child's apostasy should reach her ears.
For Photo was the general favourite with
young and old. Each mother wished him
for the husband of her daughter, and
many a young maiden's heart secretly beat
at the name of Photo Tzavella.

Meanwhile, certain movements observed
among the Vezir's troops on the opposite
heights, and confirming rumours which
had previously reached them, awakened the
suspicions of Tzavella and the other Suliote
captains, that the enemy meditated ere
long an assault on their advanced post.
Preparations for defence were accordingly
made; men were posted at the different
points from which the approach of the
assailants could be most distinctly observed. Signals were agreed upon to give
notice of danger, and the spots were
selected which overlooked the paths by
which the enemy must necessarily ascend
to the assault, and whence the women,

secured by the natural parapets of the rocks, might assist in the defence by rolling down upon the Turks fragments of rock and stone, which were heaped in abundance upon the edge of the over-hanging precipices.

As the day advanced, the lowering appearance of the sky, the oppressive sultriness of the veiled atmosphere, gave warning of a storm being abroad some-where. The watchers were enjoined re-doubled vigilance, lest the enemy, like the wild beasts of the forest, taking advantage of the darkness and confusion which the sudden outbreak of the storm might bring with it, should, under cover of it, come upon them unawares. The day, however, passed on without any notable change, either in the sky or in the hostile camp; and so, about the time of sunset, when the beat of the sounding-board, the Hellenic gong, gave notice of evening prayer, the lowly church was filled with a congregation now consisting principally of the women, the armed men being for the greater portion absent at the posts assigned them in the earlier part of the day by their chiefs.

In addition to the usual service, the Papàs, old Anthimos, offered up a prayer for the protection of the common fatherland, and then, instead of the usual blessing, with which he was accustomed to dismiss his flock, he, with unusual solemnity, called upon them to join in the anathema which he pronounced upon any who in the approaching conflict with the bloody Turks should be so base as to turn traitors and renegades, to save their own lives or to purchase an infamous reward from the sworn enemies of their faith.

A deep and hearty Amen from the whole congregation responded to the awful curse; and none so deep and so hearty as from the wife of Tzavella. The anathema of the old priest seemed to be ratified from heaven by a loud thunder-clap, announcing the arrival of the storm that had been threatening all the day.

As the women were hurrying out of the church to their homes, Mosco heard one say to another —

" Who are the traitors and renegades Papàs Anthimos has been cursing ? There are none such among us."

A voice replied, " What ! have you not heard the news that Tzavella's son has turned Turk ? "

At that moment a flash of lightning showed to the shuddering mother the face of the last speaker. She recognised the hard features of one who had been her rival for her husband's love, and who had never forgiven her.

Another voice instantly retorted, " 'Tis false ! " and at the same time Mosco felt her hand seized and pressed to lips that glowed with the fervent deprecation of the baseness imputed to her son.

" Who art thou, my child ? " said she.

But the loud raving of the storm, which

had now begun in earnest, intercepted the answer. She only caught the momentary glimpse of a young girl's face, which seemed to the grateful mother's distracted heart as it had been one of the heavenly host proclaiming peace from above.

Lambro Tzavella was engaged in consultation with the other captains when his wife reached the Pyrgo, where they were assembled.

Hearing many voices within, she sat down on the threshold of the half-opened door, in the midst of the pelting of the storm. The storm of her own perturbed spirit made her heedless of that which raged without.

In the intervals between the bursting of the thunder-clouds, Mosco caught the sound of Photo's name as it was mentioned by one of the speakers. The pulses of her heart ceased, while she strained her ears to listen, anxious, yet dreading to learn what was being said of her son.

" Well, if it were not he I saw in the

suite of Vely Pasha, as he stood examin-
ing our advanced position this morning
with his glass, it was so like him that they
might easily be taken one for the other."

" Selim Bey, the Vezir's grandson, is, -
I have been told, very like Photo, and of
the same height, though younger. He it
was, perhaps, whom you saw. For my
part, I never will believe that any Suliote
child, much less a son of Lambro Tza-
valla's, could be base enough to renounce
his faith from fear of death."

The mother's heart yearned to thank
the generous assertor of her boy's innocence; but as she rose from her lowly
seat, hesitating whether or not to intrude
into the council, the chiefs took their
leave of Tzavella, and hurried away for
the execution of what had been determined upon among them. When they
were all departed, Mosco ventured into
the room, at the other end of which was
seated her husband, so immersed in
thought that he seemed to be uncon-

scious of her presence. It was only when she had lighted a small lamp, which hung against the wall, that Tzavella was aware of his wife's presence.

" Thou art drenched, woman," said he; "thou hast been exposed to the storm. Light a fire and warm thee."

" Think not of such trifles now," said Mosco. " I have a fire burning here which will consume my heart unless———. Tell me, Lambro, hast thou heard any tidings of our Photo?" and she looked steadfastly and keenly into her husband's eyes, as if to detect any discord between his look and the answer she expected.

Lambro did hesitate to reply.

" Speak, Lambro, or I die at thy feet."

" I *have* heard tidings of my son, which, rather than they prove true, I would see him lying dead on that floor."

" And dost thou, then, believe them to be true? That boy who sucked, with the milk from this bosom, the hatred of the Turk; who, from a child, showed himself so fearless, and yet so gentle; so bold, and yet so tender-hearted — dost thou not remember how he watched by his brother's bedside, and how he strengthened him in his last agony, young as he was, with words of faith, — can he be a renegade? Impossible ! — impossible !"

She paused for a moment, and then added, in a solemn, deliberate tone, without a tear or a faltering tongue,—

" Hear me, Tzavella. Were it possible that a child of mine could be guilty of such wickedness, I would, with these hands, which pressed him to my bosom when as yet he knew not the difference between good and evil, Christian and Turk, I would tear out his renegade tongue by the root and dash it in his face."

The unhappy mother, exhausted by her passion, and recoiling from her own unnatural energy, burst into a deluge of tears, and clasped her husband in her arms, and, sobbing, repeated,—" Impossible ! — impossible !"

How many hearts would break, made brittle by the scorching heat of adversity, but for those fountains of the eyes, mercifully designed to soften and relieve the anguish that causes them to flow!

Tzavella did not attempt to restrain his wife's tears.

"I was consulting with the other captains," said he, after a short pause, during which he appeared busied with his arms; "the Turks will, I expect, attack us early to-morrow."

"Thou wilt let me be with thee," interrupted Mosco, wiping away her tears. "I know how to load a toufenk, and, if need be, to fire one off."

"Yes," said Tzavella, kissing away the drops that still lingered on her cheeks, "thou shalt be at my side, and share my dangers, brave Suliotissa as thou art."

"Promise me one thing," said she. "Should'st thou chance to take Aly's grandson alive,—that boy they call Selim, — thou wilt deliver him into none other hands but mine. I've heard that the tyrant doats on the boy."

Mosco looked earnestly into her husband's eyes, and added, " Thou understandest ?"

" I understand," answered the chief.

" Thou dost promise me, then ?"

" I promise."

Had Alỳ witnessed the cruel glance which shot from that woman's eyes as she spake, he had trembled at the bare thought of his favourite child falling at that moment into her hands.

Oh ! what fiendish schemes of deadly revenge may take root in the noblest natures, when galled and exasperated by long years of oppression ! Who can wonder, if fortune presents the sweet poison to the lips of the oppressed, that they drink it to intoxication ?"

" Blood for blood—woe for woe !" is the natural cry of the soul, maddened and brutalised by the scorpion whips of the oppressor.

CHAPTER XLIX.

THE day had hardly broke after that tempestuous night, when all the fighting population of Suli were already at the posts assigned them by their leaders, in expectation of the threatened assault.

There was one point somewhat in advance of the general line of defence occupied by the Suliotes, jutting out against the Turkish camp, like a fist thrust insultingly into an opponent's face, which it was essential to the success of the ulterior operations of the besiegers not to leave in possession of the besieged. The position resembled that of the Philistine garrison invaded by Jonathan and his armour-bearer. There was a sharp rock on the one side, and a sharp rock on the other side, and between them was a deep ravine, at the bottom of which ran the path that led to the outlet from this labyrinth of dells into the plain of the Glykys Limen.

It was here that Tzavella and his men were posted, impatiently waiting for the tardy daylight, which struggled to find its way into the deep valleys through the lazy masses of clouds that were sleeping, pillowed on the mountain tops, as if fatigued with the tempests of the night.

As soon as the surrounding objects began to be partially discernible, Tzavella fired a shot in the direction of the opposite rock, across the hollow which divided the hostile parties, as a signal to the different Suliote posts to be on the alert.

The shot was presently responded to by several shots fired from the other side, which being heard to strike against the face of the rock where Tzavella stood, gave certain evidence of the proximity of the marksmen; but the numbers and position of the enemy were still concealed from view by the grey mists which hung in wreaths along the sides of the hill.

The sound of the shots, repeated by the echoes from every rock and cavern, had hardly died away before all the women of Suli, the wives, mothers, and sisters of its defenders, were by the side of each, ready to take their share in the common peril.

None but the very aged and infirm, and the young children, were absent. These were removed to places of shelter at the highest part of the rocky citadel of Trypa, beyond the reach of the assailants' fire. Some of the elders of the younger fry could, however, with difficulty be persuaded to reckon themselves among the non-combatants, squeaking out with their tiny voices that they were quite old enough to fight—young Hannibals, taught by their mothers, from their birth, to hold in utter contempt, and to vow eternal enmity against those *gaïdhouria*—those asses of Turks.

Tzavella's wife was not the last of that heroic company to be at the post of danger; nor did she come empty-handed; for, besides bringing in the skirts of her garment a heap of cartridges which she had assisted in making up, she bore on her head a bundle, which, with those munitions of war, she cast upon the ground at her husband's feet.

"There, Lambro," she said, "I have brought thee wherewithal to despatch some scores of those Turks yonder, and somewhat besides to bind up the wounds of our Palikaria."

The bundle contained every article of her own scanty wardrobe, cut up into strips fit for bandages — a poor and worthless sacrifice, perhaps, in the eyes of those who merely give out of their superfluity useless baubles, jewels of silver and jewels of gold, but, like the widow's mite, precious in the sight of whoever estimates the value of the sacrifice by the self-devotion of the offerer.

" But I must have something in return for these," said Mosco. " I have nothing to defend myself with, if they succeed in getting up here."

" That's but fair," replied Tzavella : " take this pistol ; 'tis loaded ; only reserve thy fire till thou hast thy foe within arm's length of thee, and aim straight at his heart."

While they were yet speaking the whole landscape, hitherto shapeless, changed as if touched by the wand of an enchanter. The torpid mists below, set in motion by the fresh morning breeze,—the herald of the unwearied giant that ever rejoices to run his daily course, — were rolled up as a scroll and melted out of sight. The upper clouds, too, that looked so impenetrably solid as hardly to be distinguished from the mountain-peaks they rested on, reddened with the increasing light, and then slunk away, like guilty things, before the face of jocund day.

" There's something moving in the

valley down yonder," shouted a Palikari, who was on the look-out from a spot above the plateau, where Tzavella and his men were stationed.

"What do they look like?"

"There are loaded mules."

"Never mind the mules," cried the chief impatiently. "How many men are there? Are they armed?"

"No: they appear to be traders."

"Be they friends or foes," said Lambro, girding on his sword, and snatching up his gun, "they must pay toll to us before they do to the Vezir; our needs just now are greater than his."

"You must be quick then, Captain," cried the vedette Palikari; "the Turks are moving down upon them."

"Say'st thou so? Then we must be beforehand with those dogs."

The instinctive greed of the indigent mountaineers could not resist the temptation of plunder, for which indeed there was in this case a plausible excuse, in the extremity to which they were in danger of being reduced by lack of provisions.

" We shall soon be back, woman," said Tzavella, turning to his wife. " Do thou meanwhile watch the movements of the enemy over the way. They will not venture to climb up on this side; if they should attempt it, push those stones down upon them: that will be enough to stop them."

" Follow me, Palikaria."

In a few moments Tzavella and his men were out of sight, like eagles swiftly flying to the quarry.

Mosco felt not a little anxious when, finding herself alone with none but women like herself, she reflected on the defenceless state in which this important point, the key of the Suliote position, was thus improvidently left by its garrison, with the enemy at the door.

There were but two paths by which this summit was accessible, both narrow, abrupt, and stony,—the one by which

Tzavella and his band had just descended into the valley, the other almost precipitous, which debouched into the deep ravine at the foot of the opposite position occupied by a detachment of Alỳ Pasha's troops. In this path, or rather cornice, there was a sudden turn, a little below the summit, capable of being defended by a few resolute men against any number of assailants. But what if the Vezir's troops were to attempt an irruption on this side, while there was not one man to defend it?

Tzavella's wife had heard this discussed more than once between her husband and the other captains. But the brave woman was not disheartened, nor did she betray any alarm to her companions.

After a few moments' deliberation with herself, she called them around her, and said, "Our Palikaria have left us to ourselves for a short space, while they are gone to get a supply of provisions for us and for our——" her voice faltered as she added, "children."

"They will soon be back; but lest those Turks yonder should try to get up here before our husbands are here to fight them, we must manage as well as we can without them. Do you keep watch upon the brink, to see whether anything stirs below, while I go and see what our men are doing on the other side."

As the women stationed themselves according to the Capitanessa's directions near the edge of the precipice, along which heaps of stones and fragments of rocks were piled, ready for action, Mosco clambered over the rough ground which separated the spot from the pinnacle whence she had been accustomed to look out for her Photo. She had nearly reached it when the tinkling of a tiny bell drew her attention to a kid that was browsing among the rocks; and she saw, a little further on, climbing up by the same steep path, a young girl, to whom the little animal, alarmed at the approach of a stranger, bounded away for shelter.

"What has happened? What art thou afraid of?" said the child to her pet: and turning her head back, she saw Mosco, who immediately recognised the lovely, loving face whose look had cheered her the night before in the middle of the storm.

"What art thou doing here, child, all alone," said Mosco, "while all else are gathered together, either for battle or for shelter? Thou art too young to be exposed to the peril of arms. Why hast thou not remained with the rest?"

"I have nobody to care for me, except this poor little dumb creature," answered the girl; "and Papàs Anthimos. When he heard the shots fired just now, he sent me to come up here and see what it was about, and bring him back news at the church. Papàs Anthimos is old and nearly blind, you know, and he calls me his little daughter."

"Well, then, we will go together," said

Mosco; "and henceforth I will be a mother to thee, for the word thou spakest to me last night."

The girl looked up in Mosco's face, her eyes sparkling with gratitude, and kissed her hand.

" From this moment thou art my daughter," said Mosco; and a mutual embrace ratified the heart's covenant between them.

They had now reached the height which commanded the view of the vale beneath, and the young maiden, at a bound, was standing as dauntless and steady as a chamois on the highest pinnacle of the overhanging crags.

Her first exclamation quickened the pace and the heart-pulse of Mosco.

" Oh! look. There's something going to happen. See how all those mules are running different ways, scattered and frightened. Look! look! the Turks are rushing on the men; and now the men are standing still, as if they were afraid to meet them, and were crying *Amàn!* They are running away!"

Mosco was presently at her side; and, like her, straining her eyes, her heart-strings ready to snap with the intensity of the emotions caused by the sight of what she saw.

"*Kyrie eleyson!* The Turks are beforehand with our Palikaria, and are more than twice as many! See! they have come up with the men. O Panayï-amou! what will become of us?"

"See! see!" cried Phrosyne (so the young girl was called), "the men have stopped. Look! they have thrown off their cloaks. Don't you see the flash of their pistols? and now they have drawn their swords. They are friends! they are friends!" and she clapped her hands with joy. "They are Palikaria, and brave ones, too. Now they are all mingled together. Some are fallen to the ground. The Turks are too many for them. Oh, what a dreadful sight!"

The two spectatresses shrieked, trembling with terror. They covered their faces with their hands, longing, and yet not daring to watch the progress of the fight.

Presently a shout was heard, which made them look up, and Tzavella and his band, who had hitherto been concealed from their view by a spur of the hill, at the foot of which lay their march, emerged into sight, and were now clearly discerned rushing with their swords drawn to the scene of action.

Mosco uttered a scream of mingled exultation and alarm as she saw her husband, followed by the rest, plunge into the thick of the *mêlée*.

" See ! see !" exclaimed Phrosyne, again clapping her hands, " see ! the Turks are now hemmed in by the Palikaria on both sides ! Look ! how many are falling under the Suliotes' swords !"

" Oh that my Photo were at his father's side !" cried Mosco.

And now a cry as of triumph was

raised, returned by all the echoes round, while such of the Turks who succeeded in slipping out of the fray were seen clambering up the steep sides of the opposite hill, and making for the Pasha's head-quarters.

Some of them, as they fled, were seen to drop at the fire of the Palikaria.

The attention of Mosco and of her young companion was so rivetted upon the exciting spectacle, that they both started as from a dream on seeing one of the women, who had been left to watch on the other side, clambering up the rocks all pale and breathless, with only strength enough left to say, " The Turks! the Turks ! "

" Well, what of the Turks?" answered Mosco, endeavouring to conceal under a show of indifference the alarm she felt at the peril foreshadowed in those words. But her presence of mind did not forsake Tzavella's wife, and her courage was sustained by the thought of the success she had just been eye-witness of, achieved by her husband.

As she hurried down to return with the messenger to the post of danger she said to Phrosyne,—

" Do thou go and station thyself at the top of the path by which our Pali-karia will soon be coming up, and bid them hasten to our assistance."

" I will run and meet them half-way," replied the young girl; and followed by the kid, was presently out of sight.

On Mosco's joining her companions, she learned the full extent of the danger. The Vezir's troops were assembled at the foot of the crag, and some few had begun to ascend. The stones which had been rolled down had not deterred them, for the invaders were protected by the pro-truding angles of the zig-zag rocks, and such missiles had no chance of taking effect till they reached the upper portion of the path which led up directly to the brink where the last stand was to be made.

While the women were deliberating what was to be done, a shout from beneath was heard; and Mosco, looking down, perceived, to her dismay, the cruel faces of the dreaded assailants upturned towards her, who had just got footing on the path at that critical turn whence their further ascent was no longer to be arrested by the very inefficient means possessed by the defenders.

There stood, inclined upon the very verge of the precipice near which they were huddled together, a huge fragment of loose rock, but far too massive for such feeble arms to endeavour to displace.

Oh! for an angel's strength to roll down that stone on the heads of their enemies, and save those poor defenceless women from the fate, worse than death, that awaited them, if those merciless invaders should succeed in reaching that height, where they had fancied themselves so secure!

They look at one another in blank

despair. " Had we but arms to defend ourselves!"

The shouts and yells of the approaching foe sounded nearer and nearer.

" At least," cried Mosco, drawing from her girdle the pistol given her by Tzavella, " I will hush one of those shouters;" and she was within a pace of the fatal brink, when a strange, hollow, fearful sound was indistinctly heard, as of very distant thunder, but not from the sky above. It could hardly be called a sound, but as it were the *fore-echo* of one, like one of those unaccountable presentiments of coming events which suddenly rush into the minds of men, they know not how or whence.

At the same instant, with no greater interval than that which intervenes between the lightning's flash and the thunder-bolt shot from a cloud right overhead, an aguish trembling shook the solid ground, the women instinctively shrunk back from the dangerous spot where they stood, and tottered away from it in terror, with the uncertain steps of those who pace the heaving deck of a ship in a storm. Another moment, and the huge stone was observed to nod, topple over, and was then heard rolling and thundering down into the deep ravine beneath, crashing every obstacle, animate or inanimate, in its way.

Wailings, and groanings, and shriekings, as of living beings in a death-struggle, mingled with the echoes of the terrific avalanche, and continued to be heard, fainter and fainter, long after these had subsided.

The women looked at each other in the bewilderment of fear and joy. They hardly believed the evidence of their own senses that that great immovable stone was no longer there.

Tzavella's wife was the first to venture to approach the edge where it had stood, and when she ascertained by her own observation the extent of the catastrophe caused by the earthquake, she called her companions together, and they all fell on their knees, and with uplifted hands and eyes thanked God for their wonderful deliverance. "Surely it was a miracle!" said one to the other. "What else could have saved us? Blessed be the Panayïa and the holy saints!"

The sight which Mosco saw as she looked down into the ravine was indeed a fearful one.

The path which a few minutes before was alive with truculent eyes flashing with the lust of blood no longer existed. Instead, there was an impassable chasm. The edge of it, and the face of the rock that overhung it, was crimsoned and wet with blood. Fragments of human limbs were hanging by shreds to the sharp points of the jagged rocks, and far beneath heaps of bodies, crushed and flattened by the ruin, filled up the stony channel of the ravine; and the plashes of water, left by the storm of the preceding night, were tinged with the human gore which oozed from the still breathing but senseless mass.

As Mosco turned away from the sickening sight she was startled by a moan, and looking again, she perceived, clinging to a jutting piece of rock, a short space below the edge, one solitary survivor of the wreck. He was looking upwards, seeking for a support on which to fasten his hands, and if possible to lift himself to a spot promising a surer footing than that on which he was, as it were, suspended over the yawning void below him. The sweat was upon his brow, and his strength was all but gone. As he looked up his eyes met Mosco's, who then perceived that he was a mere boy, younger than her own Photo. But there was in the expression of his beautiful features a manly spirit, which seemed to be contending against the suffering of recent exertion, beyond his years, and present danger, and Mosco felt in the glance of his beseeching, yet not

timorous eye, an appeal to her womanly
tenderness, which it was impossible to
resist.

She called to him with an encouraging
voice not to fear, and then with the assistance of the other women, who twisted
several of their girdles together into a
stout cord, and giving him directions
where to place his hands and feet, contrived to haul him up and land him safe
on the inside of that natural battlement.

This was not effected without some difficulty and risk, and the lad was so exhausted by the efforts he had made to
hold his ground, that the women at first
apprehended he had not long to live.

While they stood round him they had
leisure to remark the richness of his
clothing.

" He is all over gold embroidery," they
observed one to the other.

" Everything is so new and clean, it's
the first time, I dare say, he has left his
mother to fight with enemies."

" Ah ! " observed another, " if his mother knew what had happened to him ! "

After a while the young Turk came to himself, and it was with a mingled feeling of shame and anger that he found himself the gazing-stock of so many eyes, bent upon him with curiosity and childish wonder. A lion's whelp entrapped in ignoble toils, and stared at with impunity by a herd of does and fawns, could not feel more awkward than did this unfledged little despot at being thus stared at.

When he could bear it no longer, he started upon his feet, and looking round with a haughty eye and scornful lip, abruptly asked,—

" Did you never see a man before ? "

The women shrank back as if a wild cat had leaped into the midst of them.

Mosco alone treated his airs with haughtiness equal to his own.

" Child ! " she said, in a tone which sounded like an ironical comment upon his disdainful question, "thou art *my* captive — I have saved thy life; and now tell me, what hast thou to offer for thy ransom?"

"Woman," replied the Moslem boy, "a Vezir's grandson does not surrender to any but armed men. Had I not lost my arms, *they* should not have taken me alive."

"Thou art of that vile Toshki brood, then? Thou hadst better have cut out thy tongue, child, than tell me that. I am the mother of Photo Tzavella, — knowest thou *that*, thou child of the bloody Vezir? I have been praying, day and night, that one as dear to him as my child is to me (but that can never be!) might fall within my grasp; and now that I have thee, thinkest thou that I will accept of any ransom? No; if thy accursed grandfather were to give me his palace full of diamonds, he shall never see thy face again. I thank God, the day of revenge is at last arrived!"

There was something inexpressibly fearful in the shriek of frenzied delight with which this tender mother thus uttered her thanksgiving to the compassionate Father of all his creatures at the opportunity of slaking her thirst for vengeance in the blood of an innocent victim.

Bold and courageous as the young Selim Bey had shown himself, he was abashed, not to say frightened, at the dreadful expression of the Suliote woman's countenance and the unnatural tones of her voice. The other women, — some of whom had lost sons in the wars with Alỳ Pasha, — at the sight of Mosco's fury, they too kindled with passion ; and there is no saying whether the boy might not have shared the fate of Orpheus among the Bacchanals had not their attention been suddenly attracted to another object by the sound of shots and the exultant cries of the Suliotes, as they ascended the path from the scene of their recent conflict with the Turks, escorting the few prisoners whom they had spared, and accompanied by their Klephtic allies. They were heralded by Phrosyne, who, as she came bounding like a fawn to Mosco, cried,—" He's come! Photo is come!"

Mosco heard the words, but did not seem to understand their meaning. She turned her head back to see, incredulous from joy and wonder, and in the next moment was locked in her son's embrace.

Both were speechless for a while, and when at length the fulness of their hearts found a vent in language, the only words that first rose to their lips were,—" My own dear child!"—" My dear, darling mother!"

As Photo recovered from the first emotion of this meeting his eye caught sight of the figure of young Selim, who was standing apart, and quite alone (for all the women had hurried away to meet the returning Palikaria), looking across the ravine towards his own people.

Mosco answered the question which

she detected in Photo's look before his tongue gave it utterance.

"That is *my* prisoner, Photakimou," she said, triumphantly. "He must pay dearly for his ransom, and I will give him a taste of the cup thou hast been made to drink by his tyrant grandfather."

"Say'st thou so, mother?" said Photo. "Is that really Selim Bey, the only being whom, they say, that cruel Pasha loves?"

"Even so, my child; and if that monster has a heart, he shall be made to feel what it is to torture a mother's heart. His child shall pay for what mine was made to endure."

"Not so, dearest mother, if you love me," said Photo, tenderly kissing her cheek. "You will not harm that boy, when you know that he it was who, alone of all the Pasha's people, begged for my life, when I was doomed to die. Oh! mother, if a hair of that child's head is touched, and I stand by without defending him, I shall feel myself disgraced for ever. I could not thank him then — I *must* do so now."

Photo approached Selim, who was still gazing despondingly on the opposite hills, where he could see the shattered remains of the defeated party slowly and painfully ascending.

At the sound of Photo's step the young Turk turned his head, but did not recognise him. Photo would have taken his hand, but he held proudly back.

" You don't recollect the Suliote captive condemned to die, whom you would have saved," said Photo. " But *he* has never forgotten your generous intercession in his behalf. It was not my fault if I did not thank you then. I would now show my gratitude by more than mere words. You are a captive as I was, but by what chance I have not yet learnt. All I care to know is how to spare you the sufferings which I endured."

Young Selim's Moslem pride had made him hard in the presence of the women.

Mosco's taunts and threats, so far from mollifying him into submission, caused him to set his face as a flint against every torment their malice could devise; but when left alone to turn his thoughts on his present condition, so fatally the reverse of what in his young ambition he had anticipated that morning, when he aspired to lead the assault against Suli,—his first prowess in arms,—his heart sunk in utter despondency. No wonder, then, that the kind words of Photo, striking on it at that moment, like the Prophet's rod upon the flinty rock, made the waters flow. The poor captive, overpowered by the unexpected sympathy of a young and noble heart like his own, threw his arms round Photo's neck, and the two youths, like David and Jonathan, kissed one another, and wept one with another, till they could weep no longer.

The only witnesses of this scene were Mosco and Phrosyne—Mosco felt herself rebuked by the language of her generous son to her prisoner, and when she beheld that burst of tenderness in the stripling who but a few moments since she had seen so haughtily defiant of her rage, proving that even the hated Turk had a touch of humanity in his composition no less than the Greek, all her thoughts of vengeance vanished, and she could not refrain from tears of pity.

" Why," said she, addressing herself to Selim with a voice of gentle reproach, nay almost of humble apology, which singularly contrasted with the bitterness of her former words,—" Why, μωρὲ παιδὶ, did you not tell me that you had been so friendly to my son when he was in like distress? Do you suppose I could have shut my ears to such a plea?"

The boy tossed up his head proudly, passed his hand over his eyes, as if ashamed of having given way to tears before a woman.

" Because you and those women would

have thought I was afraid to die—that's why. If it is my Kismet to die, *Allah Ekber!*—God is great."

The dialogue was interrupted by the approach of Lambro Tzavella, accompanied by Samuel and Dhimo. As Mosco ran to meet her husband, she perceived his sleeve to be soaked with blood from a gash across his arm. To the anxious look with which she accosted him, he replied, "'T is a mere trifle, woman; if no worse befell me in our skirmish just now, we have to thank our brave Photaki. It was he saved my life, before I knew he was near. But for him I should not have been here to tell thee, nor but for these two faithful friends, would thy child have been at hand to defend his father's life against the knife of the Turks."

"The joys of parents are secret, and so are their fears and griefs: they *cannot* utter the one, nor will they not utter the other."

Thus speaks the English sage, who had been ranked with the seven wise men of Greece had he lived in their days.

And so it was with the father and mother of our hero, as they alternately pressed him to their bosom in speechless delight. They *could* not utter their joy.

Photo did not, in the fond embraces of his parents, forget the interests of the captive Selim. His own happiness only made him more generously mindful of the contrast between it and the desolateness of his friend, and he felt still more keenly alive to it when he noticed the curious and hostile glances exchanged between the Chief and the old Caloyero, as they first perceived the young Turk standing near and Phrosyne by his side.

The young Suliote maiden was trying to cheer him with kind words, for all her compassion had been roused in his behalf when she learned how he had befriended Photo in his need.

" He is *my* prisoner," said Mosco to

her husband, in reply to his inquiry for an explanation of what had occurred during his absence from the spot.

" Well, woman," said Tzavella, " thou hast achieved a greater victory than we men, and thou must do what thou wilt with thine own."

He turned a threatening look upon Alỳ Pasha's grandson, and added,—

" I made thee a promise last night. I now fulfil it. • I leave thy prisoner to thy mercy. Take him, and do what thou wilt with him."

Photo here interposed, and taking Selim by the hand, he addressed his mother,—

" Dear mother, I claim your captive as my reward for what you heard my father say of me just now. Surely you will not refuse your son that boon which I crave of you in behalf of one who so generously interposed to save my life?"

He then turned to his father and to Samuel, and pleaded the cause of the young Turk with all the fervent eloquence of a confiding young heart that, in its noble illusions, knows no difference of race or creed, but fondly dreams that the hard, selfish world, is to be overcome by loving it.

Would the affairs of the world indeed go worse if the rigidity of its politic rules were sometimes relaxed by a slight alloy of generous feeling?

Mosco looked with a wistful eye to the two men, who remained silent while Photo was speaking. Phrosyne drank in every word, as if it came from the lips of an angel. Selim's heart was knit to his for ever.

Samuel broke the silence. As if he had taken no notice of Photo's pleading, he turned to Mosco,—

" Did not I tell thee, woman, that thy son should be restored to thee? I have been better than my word. In Photo thou hast not only thy son, but a Palikari, —παλικαρᾶτος, the bravest of the brave."

" But, brave as thou art, Photo," continued the rough old man, " thou art yet young, and must leave matters of counsel that concern the commonweal to thy elders. *They* must decide as to the disposal of the prisoners.

" But we must first all go and praise the God of Battles for the victory. Henceforth the Suliote war-cry shall be, ' The Sword of Photo ! ' "

FINIS.

A FEW remarks on the changes which have occurred in the state of things in Turkey since the
date of this story, now more than half a century
old, may, perhaps, find favour with the reader
who feels an interest in the future destinies of
that country, one of the fairest portions of the
globe.

Those changes are great and notorious; they
are matters of recent history; they are passing
under our own eyes with a rapidity which baffles
all calculation, and there is not one of them
which is not tending more or less directly to the
dissolution of the old Ottoman system : changes
in the forms of administration; changes in the
court etiquette; changes in dress; changes in
social intercourse with foreigners, — witness the
appearance of the Sultan, *K.G.!* at a ball given
by Queen Victoria's Ambassador—a fact which is
of itself *almost* a revolution.

So far these changes seem to indicate what is
called *progress,* but it is such progress as a traveller makes who is floundering by night in a

quagmire, out of which when he has extricated himself, he may perchance find that he is on the edge of a precipice.

Such, in fact, would seem to be the present condition of the Turkish empire—a state of transitiou from the old *dis*order of things to an unknown future; where all is confusion and uncertainty, like one of the dissolving views' seen at the moment when the first picture is beginning to vanish, and the second has not yet emerged into light, and both are still so blended as to perplex the spectator by the indistinctness of the receding and the approaching objects.

This confusion was the inevitable and foreseen result of the agitation of the Eastern Question, and of the fierce and short struggle which ensued at the gates, as it were, of the Sultan's palace. It was impossible but that the sudden irruption into the Turkish capital and provinces of such a stream of foreigners of various races, British, French, Sardinians; of soldiers, sailors, civilians, and *hospital nurses*, coming into hourly contact with the natives, under entirely novel circumstances, must have been accompanied by a corresponding influx into the minds of thousands of new ideas and notions, which must be actually fermenting and preparing the development of some great providential purpose which we may presume God has in view when His judgments are made manifest upon the earth. The late war was the ploughshare to break up the soil, and prepare it for the new seed which is to be cast into the furrows. Great is the responsibility of those on whom that work devolves. Time only will show the fruit; but there is one effect of the war already ascertained, and one of no little importance in the consideration of the subject, namely, that it has laid bare to the knowledge of the whole world, of friends as well as of foes, the inveterate vices and defects of the Turkish system of government; and, in contrast with these, has brought into light the good, sterling qualities of the Turkish *people*.

On the one hand, in the people is found a natural probity and simplicity of character, sobriety, courage, patient endurance, docility, attachment to those who obtain and deserve their confidence.

On the other hand, the character of the Turkish official, high and low, is marked by intrigue, venality, corruption, profligacy, sensuality too revolting to be even alluded to, polluting every channel of the public administration, and opposing insurmountable obstacles to the success of every attempt at reform, which would interfere with the indulgence of the most detestable vices of the rulers and their subordinates.

" Imported slaves fill many places in the state, and most places in private families, which might be better occupied by free natives. So placed, they minister to those habits of expense and sensuality which undermine the strength of the empire, and convey but too often the sentiments of a slave into posts of high command and honourable trust." *

In this short sentence the experienced Statesman, who is the best acquainted with the Turkish Government, discloses the real cause of those corruptions which it has been the labour of his public life, and a chief employment of his rare abilities, to combat.

Such, then, is the character of the persons coming under the abstract term of the Sublime Porte, who have by the Treaty of Paris been formally admitted to participate in the advantages of the public law and system of Europe—the same treaty by which the Christian Powers renounce the

* The Parliamentary Blue Book, Class B: The Slave Trade, 1854–5. See, at p. 607, Lord Stratford de Redcliffe's "admirable" instruction to Mr. Pisani respecting the trade in Circassian and Georgian Slaves, dated 9th August, 1854.

right, " in any case, to interfere, either collectively or separately, in the relations of the Sultan with his subjects, or in the internal administration of the empire."

Here it is that the real difficulties of the so-called Eastern Question begin — a question of which the final settlement is but one of the many problems destined, perhaps, to task to the utmost the abilities, and to perplex the speculations, of statesmen and politicians yet unborn.

The first point of that question, which was simply whether the Czar was to be the *sole* arbiter thereof, was decided at Sebastopol. Now *all* the Christian Powers have a voice in the matter, or rather they are all excluded by their own act, above cited, from any voice at all. They *make believe* that Turkey is a living body, capable of itself of performing all the functions of life, and attribute to that foul and decrepit institution, called the Sublime Porte, because washed over with a thin varnish of modern civilization, the capacity of self-regeneration.

But they who believe that Christian truth is the only instrument of national as of individual regeneration, that from it alone proceeds the breath which can animate the dry bones, will conceive hopes of a better solution of the Turkish problem from the knowledge that an element of reform has been for some years at work in the Turkish dominions, the effects of which have only begun to be perceptible since the war.

Long before the agitation of the Eastern Question, (about twenty-five years ago,) "the American Board of Commissioners for Foreign Missions" had established at Constantinople a mission with special reference to the Armenian Christians. Is it presumptuous to affirm, that the labours of the missionaries were directed by the wonderful providence of God to prepare for results far beyond what was originally contemplated by them, of which the most important has been the formal recognition by the Turkish Government of a Protestant community, recorded in a firman giving to the civil organization of the Sultan's Protestant subjects all the stability and permanency that the older Christian communities enjoy in Turkey? This important boon, first granted in the form of a Vizieral letter, at the instance of Lord Cowley, was finally ratified and secured in November 1850 by an imperial firman, emanating from the Sultan himself, obtained by Lord Stratford de Redcliffe —a service to the cause of Christianity, the magnitude of which will only be duly appreciated when its effects shall have been fully developed;

and *then* will be universally acknowledged the eminent merits of the British representative, to whose energetic intervention under God the missionaries gratefully attribute " the many important changes for the better which have taken place in the civil and social condition of the Rayahs of Turkey." *

This official recognition of a regularly constituted Protestant community has acquired an incalculable importance, independently of its bearing upon the Christian Rayahs, from the effect which it seems to have had instrumentally in awakening the attention and conciliating the good-will of the Turks to a form of Christianity hitherto unknown to them.

Till now the Turks had viewed Christianity chiefly under the form in which it is annually exhibited by the orthodox Latin and Greek Catholics, when both parties are in the habit of assaulting each other in the holy places, consecrated by the birth and death of their common Redeemer; and when Moslem police-officers are obliged to interfere to prevent the professed

* See the Supplementary Chapter and Appendix of the Rev. H. G. O. Dwight's interesting volume, entitled " Christianity in Turkey ; a Narrative of the Protestant Reformation in the Armenian Church." Nisbet, 1854.

disciples of the Prince of Peace from shedding each other's blood on the very-spot where they believe the Saviour's blood was shed for all mankind.

But, now, it has come to pass that Turks have begun to distinguish between Protestantism and Christianity, as things totally apart; in a sense, however, the very reverse of that in which the distinction is understood at Rome.

The Turkish officials, whose position has brought them into contact with the Protestant Rayahs, (chiefly Armenians, lately joined by a few Greeks), have observed with surprise and admiration the constancy with which they suffered the persecution instigated by members of their own church, and have on more than one occasion acknowledged and eulogised the exemplary moral conduct and honourable character of this newly-constituted body.

A more satisfactory proof than this of the reality of the practical good effected, with God's blessing, by the American missionaries, could not be adduced, and it may partly account for the fact which, not quite three years ago, aroused not only their attention and solicitude but that of other watchful Christians,—the fact, namely, of a demand which has since then greatly increased for the New Testament, and religious tracts, chiefly by the Turks of Constantinople.

There is something so extraordinary and singular in this fact, that those who have been most conversant with Mahometans and their fanatical prejudices will be the least disposed to give credence to it. The Moslem, taught that his religion is the completion of divine revelation, and that the Koran is the indispensable supplement to the Hebrew and Christian Scriptures, replies to the arguments adduced to convert him to the Christian faith, that he is advanced beyond it, and that, therefore, for a Moslem to become a Christian, is not progress, but a step backward in the road to spiritual perfection.*

But of the reality of the fact itself, which has been discreetly kept in the background to prevent its becoming prematurely the topic of platform agitation in England, there is no reason to doubt.

To the common-place politician, who is content to satisfy his craving for news with the husks of contemporaneous events, and who sees in the most evident manifestations of God's providential government nothing but the play of parties and the result of chance, it may seem a matter of slight consequence that at this present moment there are Turks who not only do not refuse, as heretofore,

* *Vide* Note.

to entertain the subject of Christianity at all, but
are earnestly occupied in becoming acquainted
with the Gospel in their own tongue.

The far-sighted, thoughtful Christian statesman will, on the contrary, see in this fact an
element of reform fraught with consequences far
beyond the grasp of a mere human policy, — a
fact which can no longer be safely ignored or
neglected in any speculations or plans relating to
the future destinies of Turkey.

Let it only be considered what would be the
political as well as the social results of any mate-
rial alteration in the relative numbers of the
Mussulman and Christian populations, especially
in the Asiatic Provinces, which should be effected
by the evangelising of the Turks through the
ministry of Protestant Missionaries.

The anticipation of such an event will not appear extravagant to those who know what has
been at work in the Turkish mind for some
time back, and has only come to the surface
within the last two or three years, accounting for
and justifying the opinion expressed by an old
Turk to one of our consuls, that the time was
coming when no resource would remain to the
Sultan but to become Christian.

That the truth had begun to arrest the attention of the Turks themselves so far back as 1852, is confirmed by the formal testimony of the American Missionaries in their address to Lord Stratford de Redcliffe at that period. In it they say: " The Mohammedan population of Turkey, from the Sovereign to the peasant, are beginning to see Christianity in its purest character. In the lives of the members of fourteen Protestant churches and of other Protestant communities existing in this country, they (the Mohammedans) witness the effects of a real Christianity in the quiet, godly, truthful, and conscientious behaviour of those who profess the gospel ; *and they openly avow this difference,* so honourable to Gospel truth."

All must agree in the sentiment expressed on the same occasion by the men to whose zeal, prudence, and patience in all their proceedings, honourable testimony has been invariably borne by the British representatives, that the only true and solid basis of the prosperity and strength of the Ottoman Government itself is to be found in the civil order and social prosperity, the intellectual and moral progress of all its subjects, attendant on the extension of a pure Christianity among them.

On such a basis the independence and integrity of the Ottoman empire would more securely rest than upon the common guarantee* of Foreign Powers, *who may not always be agreed.*

To have been made an instrument in the hand of God for promoting this grandest of all objects —the extension of Christian truth in the earth— is the greatest glory a British statesman can aspire to, and it is the peculiar felicity of the position of England towards Turkey, that her own best interests are identified with the promotion of that same object in the Sultan's dominions. For the extension and prosperity of her commerce, the success of her industrial enterprises, and the profitable employment of her capital in Turkey, as well as the security and rapidity of her overland communications with her Indian empire, are all dependent on conditions implying the well being of all classes of the population of Turkey, the improvement of its internal administration, and the stability of its Government, as flowing from the same only *permanent* source of all national, not less than of individual, prosperity.

There can be no doubt that the reciprocal benefits accruing both to the Government and to the subjects of the Sultan would increase in pro-

---

* See the Treaty of Paris, March 30, 1856; Art. vii.

portion to the increase of the Protestant Christian element in Turkey. One of the political effects of such increase is too obvious to be overlooked, namely, that it must, in the same proportion, neutralize the influence of Russia over the Greek rayahs exercised through the medium of a common creed,—a result of no little importance in the view of those who reflect how greatly the independence of the Turkish Government has ever been endangered by that influence.

It is another peculiar felicity of England's position in the present juncture, that the Missionary work which has produced effects so remarkable was directed from a quarter not liable to the suspicion of political motives, such as would probably have been attributed to the English Government by those who from jealousy might have attempted to frustrate the work.

Our abstinence in this respect has been made the subject of remark in a sense which, while it absolves our Government from all suspicion of selfishness, brings out more conspicuously the immense service which has been rendered to the Protestant Christians of Turkey by their formal admission to the advantages enjoyed by the professors of other creeds. The remark alluded to is contained in the following extract from Dr.

Robinson's " Biblical Researches in Palestine:"
(vol. iii. p. 465.)

" France has long been the acknowledged protector of the Roman Catholic religion in the
Turkish empire . . . . The consequence is,
that wherever there are Roman Catholics, France
has interested partisans . . . . In the members
of the Greek Church, still more numerous, the
Russians have even warmer partisans . . . . .
Hence, wherever Russia sends her agents, they
find confidential friends and informants.

" But where are England's partisans in any part
of Turkey? Not a single sect, be it ever so
small, looks to her as its natural guardian. Her
wealth and her power are, indeed, admired; her
citizens, wherever they travel, are respected; and
the native Christians of every sect, when groan-
ing under oppression, would welcome a government established by her as a relief. Yet in this,
they would not be drawn by any positive attachment, but forced by a desire to escape from suffering. England has no party in Syria bound to
her by any direct tie.

" Far different would be the case, did there
exist in Syria a sect of Protestant Christians.
There is no other Protestant power to whom
such a sect could look for protection; nor would

they wish to look elsewhere, for England's protection, whenever granted, is known to be more efficient than any other. To secure the existence of such a sect, the English Government needs to take but a single step, and that unattended by difficulty or danger. It needs simply to obtain, for native Protestants, the same acknowledgment and rights that are granted to other acknowledged Christian sects. Such a request, earnestly made, the Turkish Government could not refuse. And were it done, but few years would probably elapse before many in Syria would bear the Protestant name; and, it is hoped, would also be sincere and cordial adherents of the Protestant faith."

The above remarks of an experienced and impartial observer (not confined to Syria, but applied to all Turkey,) will awaken reflections on the important task and correspondent responsibility which have devolved upon England, as the acknowledged protectress of the rising Protestant community in Turkey.

The practical question that hence concerns us is, in what mode her influence may be most beneficially exerted in its behalf consistently with the guaranteed independence of the Turkish Government, and the treaty engagement not to interfere in the Sultan's relations with his sub-jects, nor in the internal administration of his empire.

The course of the British Government appears plain enough;—simply to continue to aid, by honest counsels, the practical development of the principles of reform laid down in the Sultan's firman, communicated to the powers, and acknow-ledged by the Treaty of Paris, and, if possible, to inspire a living breath into the dead letter of that Eastern Magna Charta. The means to this end would appear to be, in the first instance, to supply a manifest deficiency in our foreign ser-vice in Turkey, by the multiplication of efficient agents appointed at every port and inland town of the country, especially of the Asiatic pro-vinces, which offer advantages for commercial and industrial undertakings of any kind, public or private.

The ground has already been broken by the introduction of the *matériel* of European civiliza-tion, in the shape of projects for the establishment of banks, railroads, &c., of which, when the first obstacles shall have been overcome, it is hardly possible to exaggerate the rapid transformation they may effect in every branch and form of social life, both among the Moslem and Christian populations. However elaborate and specious such projects may be in theory, their success must, as in every human institution, ultimately depend in practice, upon the individual men who have the principal share in their direction and execution. This is emphatically the case in a *quasi* new country like Turkey, particularly at this juncture.

Whoever reflects how greatly the influence of any government in foreign countries is affected by the character of the agents it employs, will feel how essential to the attainment of the reforms promised by the Sultan's firman is the selection by the British Government, through whose influence chiefly it was obtained, of efficient consular agents and others, specially trained for the service in Turkey.

It is not enough that they pass a creditable examination before the Civil Service Commissioners, or that, in addition to the usual attainments of men of average English education, they are (a thing indispensable) conversant with the languages spoken and written in the Levant; but it is essential that they uphold by their personal character and habitual conduct the reputation which England has always enjoyed in the Levant for truthfulness, integrity, plain dealing, and for that high moral bearing, so pithily expressed by the old Turk in the word applied by

him to the heroic defender of Kars — *Chok adàm*
— a *thorough* man.

It is only among the ranks of well-educated
British-born subjects, who do not depend for
their maintenance upon trade, nor are in a condition to be biassed by their. relationship with
natives, that public men of this stamp are likely
to be found.

Such men alone can secure the respect and
confidence of the Turkish provincials, (as distinguished from the corrupt foreign slave officials
before alluded to), whom it is of importance to
conciliate.

Of these, many who were recently serving
under British officers and receiving British pay
in the Turkish Contingent, Bashi Bazouks and
others, have carried back to their respective homes
a grateful recollection of the humane and generous treatment they received at the hands of
the *Ingliz Guiaoor;* and, perhaps, the seed of
Christian life, which may be now ·working in
many an honest and good heart.

These may be looked upon as the natural
partizans and admirers of England, over whom
the influence of her public agents, and of her
other subjects, who may be attracted to Turkey
by commercial, industrial, or scientific pursuits,
cannot fail to exert great influence, either in pro-

moting or obstructing the reforms which both the Turkish Government and people are equally concerned in seeing accomplished.

Who that believes in the providential super-intendence of the course of human affairs, may doubt that the exertion of British influence in an enlightened spirit of Christian policy, for which the present transitional crisis offers so remarkable an opportunity, will bring upon our Government and nation the blessing which is promised to the rulers who take counsel of God?

For the training of a class of public servants, fitted to be the instruments of such a purpose, two things are necessary: 1. Suitable institutions for their special instruction, and preparation for their public duties. 2. Sufficient funds for the establishment and maintenance of such institutions.

If some of the penny-wise legislators, who complain of the inefficiency of our foreign public servants, and yet think it a wise economy to get them *cheap*, can be persuaded to grant sufficient funds to the Government, there will be no difficulty in organising institutions of the kind. The British Protestant Colleges, already existing at Malta and Smyrna, could, under proper regulations, with the concurrence of the Foreign Department, easily be made efficiently subservient to the purpose.

A similar institution might with advantage be placed at Constantinople, where a national English Church, soon to be erected on a scale worthy of the name, and adapted to the beautiful decency of her services, will shortly open another source of Christian influence, which, under the Divine blessing, may issue in streams carrying fertility to distant regions of the East, far beyond the calculation, but not beyond the wishes, of its founders. Thus it may be hoped that the Memorial Church, besides being a monument of the national gratitude, the record of the many brave men who fell in war, will serve as a perpetual witness, in the sight of all other conflicting creeds, of the purity of our Protestant Anglican Worship, calling on them and on our own divided Church parties to adopt as their common rule of treatment towards each other, in the largest spirit of peace, the emphatically *Catholic* sentiment of the great Apostle of the Gentiles, whose own words, in their original language, would make a fitting inscription for the first English church erected in the old Greek City of Constantine and of Justinian :—

Η ΧΑΡΙΣ ΜΕΤΑ ΠΑΝΤΩΝ ΤΩΝ ΑΓΑΠΩΝ ΤΩΝ ΤΟΝ ΚΥΡΙΟΝ ΗΜΩΝ ΙΗΣΟΥΝ ΧΡΙΣΤΟΝ ΕΝ ΑΦΘΑΡΣΙΑ — "Grace be with all them who love our Lord Jesus Christ in sincerity."

NOTES TO VOL. III.

Page 3.

" Cadinn in chief to the Padishah." — " The ladies holding the first place in the Imperial harem are the Kadinns, who rank according to the date of their elevation. They are then designated *Bash* (chief) or *Buyuk* (great) *Kadinn Effendi*, second, third, and so on. . . . . These Kadinns enjoy equal rights and privileges. Their establishments are distinct, but in all respects similar. Their pin or slipper-money amounts to about 25,000 piastres per month; all other expenses are defrayed by the Sultan's treasurer." — See White's " Three Years in Constantinople, or Domestic Manners of the Turks in 1844," vol. iii. ch. i. " Imperial Harem and Household."

Page 32.

The following dialogue is meant to illustrate the mutual relations of Liberty and Equality, as understood under the *régime* referred to in the text:—

LIBERTÉ—ÉGALITÉ·

DIALOGUE.

Egalité. Ah ça, amie Liberté, tu marches trop vite; tu as deux bonnes jambes: moi, je n'en ai qu'une. Tu sais que je perdis l'autre dans les glorieuses journées, je ne me rappelle pas laquelle, il y en a eu tant. Arrête donc, que je te rattrape.

Liberté. Oh pour ça, mon amie Égalité, je ne puis t'attendre. C'est la marche du siècle et des lumières, vois tu. Je m'aperçois que tu es borgne aussi bien que boiteuse. On ne s'arrête pas dans le chemin de la perfectibilité. Je cours à la conquête du monde. Lorsque je serai arrivée au bout que voilà, je n'aurai plus à marcher, et tu pourras m'atteindre . . . . . . Or adieu, j'en suis hors, comme dit Capitaine Renard à son ami Bouc dans la fable. Que tu parviennes un peu plus tôt, un peu plus tard, c'est égal.

Egalité. Ce n'est point égal, du tout. Je ne prétends pas que tu me dévances, parbleu. Ce n'est pas comme ça que je l'entends; je ne m'appelle pas Égalité pour rien; il est convenu que nous marchions toujours d'un même pied. Ainsi, l'amie, j'insiste que tu te fasses couper une jambe et crêver un œil, sans ça . . . . . . Tu sais qu'ici il n'y a plus de *juste milieu.* Liberté, Égalité, Fraternité, ou . . . . . .

Liberté. Mais moi donc? Je ne m'appelle pas Liberté non plus pour rien, j'espère. A quoi bon avoir deux bonnes jambes, si on ne les doit utiliser que sous le bon plaisir des autres. Tant pis pour toi, si tu en as une de bois. S'il m'arrivait d'être estropiée comme toi, à la bonne heure.

Egalité. Tu le prends sur un ton fort cavalier, l'amie, mais je te rabattrai bien vite le caquet. Tu tranches du maître, tu sens même l'absolutisme. Voici la **Bourgeoise** qui vient y mettre l'ordre.

. . . Dis donc, citoyenne la camarade, entends tu cette gueuse de Liberté? elle se donne les airs de vouloir marcher toute seule, et si tu ne venais pas elle me plantait là au beau milieu du grand chemin. C'est bien à toi à décider comment la constitution l'entend, puisque c'est toi qui la fais. N'est il pas convenu que moi, Égalité, et elle, Liberté, nous devons toujours marcher fraternellement de front? Donc, Liberté n'a pas le droit de prendre les devants.

Souveraineté du Peuple. Tu as raison, camarade, ce serait donner dans le privilège, et personne n'en doit avoir, pas même la Citoyenne Liberté. Or, il est clair comme deux et deux font quatre, que deux jambes marchant plus vite qu'une seule, quand même celle-ci serait aidée de béquilles, et que deux yeux voyant plus clair qu'un seul, il n'y a plus d'égalité entre les individus. C'est du privilège tout cru ; c'est de la féodalité ; c'est l'individualisme dans toute son affreuse nudité ; c'est, enfin, violer tous les principes sortis des barricades. Or ça, nous allons trancher bien vite la question par un arrêt :—

ARRET.

Liberté, — Egalité, — Fraternité.

Nous, Souveraineté du Peuple, par la grâce de peu importe qui, Vu l'article de la nouvelle Constitution qui va se faire, et qui va déclarer que non seulement tous les français sont et resteront égaux, mais aussi que toutes les françaises seront dorénavant égales devant la loi ;

Considérant que Citoyenne Egalité n'a qu'une jambe et qu'un œil, tandis que Citoyenne Liberté est en pleine jouissance des deux espèces ;

Attendu qu'un tel état de choses n'est en harmonie ni avec la marche du siècle, ni avec le progrès des lumières, et que s'il était permis de continuer, ce serait porter un coup fatal au développement de nos institutions républicaines, mettre en péril le révolutionnement de l'ordre social, et faire désespérer de la perfectibilité du genre humain, dont nous nous sommes rendus garants ;

Arrêtons et avons arrêté ;

ARTICLE UNIQUE,

Il sera amputé une jambe et extrait un œil à la dite Citoyenne Liberté, sauf à étendre l'opération aux membres restants, si le cas échéait. Il est toutefois loisible à la dite Citoyenne de déclarer d'avance laquelle jambe et lequel œil elle préfère déposer sur l'autel de la patrie.

Notre Ministre d'Égalisation et de Justice Provisoire est chargé de l'exécution du present Arrêt.

Donné en notre Palais National des Barricades, Rue d'Enfer.

An 1 de la Liberté (bis).

Pour copie conforme,

PROCRUSTE DUNIVEAU,

Garde des Sots provisoire,
employé à la vérification
des Poids et Mesures de
la République.

Page 48.

" Beyzadé,"—literally, born of a Bey or Prince, equivalent to nobleman ; a title that used in those days to be given with little or no discrimination to all well-to-do Frengui travellers in Turkey.

Page 137.

In the " Albanesische Studien," by Dr. Johann Georg von Hahn, published at Jena in 1854, there is, at page 163 of Part I., a note entitled " Ge-

schwän-ste Menschen," or *Tailed Men*, of whom the
Doctor says, "There are two sorts, those with goat-
tails, those with small horse-tails. They who are
furnished therewith are very strong men, uncom-
monly powerful, under-built, and extraordinary
pedestrians. Two years ago there died one such,
who in one day walked a fabulous distance. The
belief in the existence of such men is not confined to Southern Albania, but extends to Greece
Proper, and even to Asia Minor. For example,
the celebrated Klepht Koutovounisios, of Lang-
kadhia, in the Morea, had a tail. Perhaps there is
more in this than a mere popular belief. One of
my Kavasses at Ioánnina, Soliman of Dragoti,
affirmed that in his part of the country men with
tails were by no means a rarity, and that he himself had a betailed cousin. .   .   .   .

"*Buffon*, in his ' Natural History,' makes mention, as I hear, of the story of there being men
with tails in Albania. Sufficient for us is the in-
disputable fact, that in Southern Albania the
people at this day believe in the existence of such
beings, as they are abundantly figured in the
representations of ancient Greece."

The Author's note on the subject concludes with
the naïve remark, that of men with the body of a
horse and the feet of a goat he had not, however,
been able to learn anything in Albania. The note
in extenso will repay the curiosity of the zoologist.

Page 139.

" 'Tis the ghost!"—In the work quoted in the preceding Note, the Author gives, at page 163, the following account of the Vourvolàk, under the head of *Gespenster.*

The belief in ghosts ("Umgehende Verstorbene," *the vagabondising defunct*) is universally spread. The Toshki Albanian calls them, as the modern Greek also does, βουρβολαx - ου (μοςμολυxειου in old Greek, the *loup-garou* of the French nursery tales). In some places it is believed that any corpse, upon which a cat or any other beast has made a spring, becomes a Vourvolàk. Such a corpse is not subject to corruption. Over its grave there is seen all night long a glimmering light; after forty days it rises and wanders about, perpetrating all manner of mischief in its own and its kinsmen's habitations, and even sleeps with the surviving wife. Formerly such corpses were dug up again and burnt, and this sometimes happens even now. This operation is performed in the night, between Friday and Saturday, at which time the Vourvolàk remains quiet in its grave. At Pcrlepé there are several families called Vampires. They are looked upon as the progeny of Vourvolàks, and are shunned by all the world. They possess the art of giving a quietus to roving Vourvolàks, — an art, however, which they keep very secret.

Page 141.

" May that drop scald thy soul!"— The same work, at p. 165, has the following : "May the drop fall upon thee!" that is, May the stroke hit thee! When, at the casting down of the rebel angels out of heaven into the abyss, the Archangel Gabriel commanded a halt, all remained immovable at the point and in the attitude in which they were at the moment when the command was given. Part of them fell beneath the earth, part lay upon the earth, while a third part remained floating above it; and hence the tears of repentance shed by these last fall upon the earth. The man upon whom drops one of these tears dies at the instant.

Page 169.

The sentiment attributed to the Bishop of Arta was shared by the celebrated Koray, well known to his countrymen for his zeal in advancing the cause of education among them, as an indispensable preliminary to their emancipation, and also to the learned of Europe by his writings, in which he aimed at the purification of the national language and mind from the corruptions contracted by both during their long subjection to the Turkish rule.

Shortly after the severance of the Greek territory from the Turkish empire, and before the establishment of the present regimen, Koray expressed to me his regret that the revolution had broke forth a generation too soon, before his countrymen were ripe for the exercise and enjoyment of freedom, and his fear lest it should issue in their subjection to a barbarian king : τις ἵνα βάρβαρον βασιλία.

Page 173.

" Σωτηρ,"—Saviour, the title appropriated in our language to our Lord, is by the modern Greek (pronounced Sotiri or Sotiris) used as a Christian name, in the same manner as its Italian equivalent, Salvator, is used by the Italians : ex. gr. Salvator Rosa.

Page 203.

I knew a Greek of one of the Ionian Islands, who was once sailing in a vessel boarded and plundered by Mainote pirates. His young bride accompanied him. In answer to a question I asked him as to the treatment they had met with, he told me that he had made up his mind, if they had attempted to offer violence to his wife, *to begin by stabbing her to the heart*, and then to kill as many of them as he could, before he was killed himself.

Page 355.

The following passage from a Mahometan author, quoted by d'Ohsson in his celebrated work, " Tableau Général de l'Empire Othoman," a classical authority in such matters, will show the reader in how far the Moslem Doctors adopt the *fact* of

Christianity :—Jesus Christ, that great prophet, was born of a Virgin by the breath of the archangel Gabriel. . . . He entered on his divine mission at the age of thirty years, after his baptism by John the Baptist in the waters of Jordan. He calls people to repentance. God gives him the power to perform the greatest miracles. He heals the lepers, gives sight to the blind, quickens the dead, walks upon the waters of the sea. . . . This Messiah of the nations thus proves his apostleship by a crowd of prodigies. The simplicity of his exterior, the humility of his conduct, the austerity of his life, the wisdom of his precepts, the pureness of his moral doctrine, are superhuman. Wherefore is he rightly called by the holy and glorious name of *Rouhh' Ullah, i. e.* The Spirit of God.—Vol. i. p. 108, octavo ed. Paris, 1788.

It is also declared by the *Imams*, or Doctors of the law, that "Christ will be the last of the universal Kaliphs, who will come at the end of time to exercise, as the vicar of Mohammed, the rights of the Priesthood, and of the supreme power over all the nations of the earth."—P. 427.

The acknowledgment of the fact, though mixed as it is with error, would seem to afford a good starting-point for religious tracts addressed to the Turks.

London :—Printed by G. BARCLAY, Castle St. Leicester Sq.

Just published, price 10*s.* 6*d.* 1 vol. post 8vo.

MAY HAMILTON,

AN AUTOBIOGRAPHY.

By JULIA TILT,

Author of " Laura Talbot," " Lays of Alma."

Just published, price 6*s.* with Thirty Illustrations,
in crown 8vo. cloth gilt,

THE CHANNEL ISLANDS, JERSEY, GUERNSEY, &c.

PICTORIAL, LEGENDARY, AND DESCRIPTIVE.

By OCTAVIUS ROOKE, Esq.

The Views in and Descriptions of the little Island of Sark
are altogether new to the Public.

" Just the book that the visitor to these Islands requires, whether he goes there to reside or pass the summer holidays. . . . . The illustrations are many of them beautiful specimens of wood engraving."—*Atlas,* June 21.

" The Channel Islands have long been left without a Guide-book. Mr. Rooke has here supplied the want in a manner that leaves nothing to be desired. This volume requires only to be known to draw to those pretty retreats a flood of visitors, who will be surprised to find they have been seeking beautiful scenery at a distance, while they have, as is too commonly the case, neglected more charming spots at home."—*United Service Magazine.*

" A most delightful volume, which, for pictorial, legendary, and descriptive illustration, may vie with any similar publication. . . . Whilst the book is practical as a guide, its introduction of history and legends renders it an instructive and entertaining companion."—*John Bull,* July 26.

" Mr. Rooke has done good service. He has made a tour of the Islands; and, finding no Guide-book to direct him, has made a very agreeable one of his own experiences These he has skilfully put together; and we see by them that he has been acute of observation, and that he has left few things pass him. He does not limit himself to topographical details, but collects legends by the way, and tells them as he passes along. These, with the general ' getting up' of the book, and numerous pictorial sketches cleverly executed, make of the whole something more than a mere ordinary Guide-book. . . . . A visitor to these Islands may do worse than take with him this volume."—*Athenæum,* August 2.

1 vol. 5*s.*

CATHEDRAL RHYMES.

Suggested by Passages in the Liturgy and Lessons.

Second Edition, price 6*d.*

ANTI-MAUD.

BY A POET OF THE PEOPLE.

" The world is wicked, and base, and vile—shall I show you a new
kind of cure?"—*Stanza II.*

Price 7*s.* 6*d.* cloth, gilt edges,

MORVEN, THE DEPARTED SPIRIT.

AND OTHER POEMS.

By R. E. S.

Price 1*s.*

THE LORD'S ANOINTED.

A Sermon preached in the British Chapel, Moscow.

By the Rev. M. MARGOLIOUTH.

(Published for the Benefit of the British Schools at Moscow.)

Lightning Source UK Ltd.
Milton Keynes UK
UKHW021937100119
335328UK00013B/1122/P